THE DSA SEASON TWO, BOOK THREE

THE MISSING

Also by Lou Paduano

The Greystone Saga

Signs of Portents

Tales from Portents

The Medusa Coin

Pathways in the Dark

A Circle of Shadows

Greystone-in-Training

Hammer and Anvil

The Gifts of Kali

The Final Gauntlet

The DSA

Season One

The Clearing

Promethean

The Bridge

Spectral Advocate

Dark Impulses

Broken Loyalties

Season Two

The Wellspring

Foundations

THE DSA SEASON TWO, BOOK THREE

 THE MISSING

Lou Paduano

Eleven Ten Publishing LLC

GRAND ISLAND, NEW YORK

Eleven Ten Publishing LLC
282 Fareway Lane
Grand Island, NY 14072

Printed in the United States of America
Edited by JP Services.
Cover art design by MiblArt

First edition published 2024

Library of Congress Cataloguing in Publication Data
Paduano, Lou
The Missing / Lou Paduano

LCCN: 2024900623
ISBN-13: 978-1-944965-41-9 (paperback)
ISBN-13: 978-1-944965-40-2 (eBook)

For Liz

CHAPTER ONE

The US-Mexico border after sunset was a wasteland. Nothing but open sky and rough terrain marked the separation between the two countries. It was a harsh landscape, filled with terrors both natural and manufactured.

Crossings occurred frequently. There was no denying it. Whether there was a wall, fence, or armed detail, people continued to travel into the deserts of New Mexico with reckless abandon. They fled violence and political strife, or because they simply needed a change.

None of it was safe. People died on the journey. Even the survivors fared no better in some regards. Their lives did not always stay their own. Too many interested parties profited off the trafficking from country to country.

Lizzy Doyle wasn't one of them. Out of the dozen shadows that flitted through the truck depot west of the Santa Teresa crossing, she was the only one trying to do something to help people.

It was no surprise to find several trucks at the depot. The closest town along the route near the border was over sixty miles away, and even then, there were few places to settle in for the night. The depot made sure truckers rested for a bit before heading to their next destination.

Some weren't traveling with commercial goods. They bore a product of a different sort. Few spoke out against the lack of regulations in the area. This was a free zone, the last true remnant of the Wild West as American's always envisioned. They rejected all government interference. They fought against anything that sought to upset their lifestyles.

That resistance led to quite a few troubling situations. It also opened the door for those willing to take advantage of their hospitality to keep the "big brothers of the border" out of their hair.

Lizzy kept low to the ground. Her camera hung from her neck, dangling in the air before her as she made her way across the crowded depot. Most of the truckers had already called it a night. One crew, however, remained on high alert. Sweeps ran along the fringes of the depot and around the gas station in the center. They moved in opposite directions, yet stayed close to the same pair of trucks at the back of the complex.

The trucks weren't registered to a company. Neither were they listed with the depot or contained a detailed manifest. The only clue to their purpose lay in the firearms at the disposal of the sentries circling the property.

Lizzy had caught wind of their arrival two days earlier. Word had come through an email from a friend down south, one she hadn't seen in years yet remembered from a brief stint in the trenches for an assignment. Her friend had barely survived an encounter with a grenade in their path, and only then, thanks to the timely intervention of Lizzy.

That had been how Lizzy made most of her contacts: through circumstances of violence and devastation. It didn't matter the danger, Lizzy had been in the thick of a number of dangerous situations to snap the relevant photo to share with the world. The friendships that developed from those moments had been merely a bonus in her eyes — but a handy one.

Lizzy left the safety of the truck on her right. She tucked tight to the front end, then shifted into the deeper shadows near the rear. The passing guards cared more for their cigarettes than any potential trouble. Lizzy was thankful for that much.

With the back of the depot cleared of personnel for the moment, Lizzy raced for the shipping container. Even through the thick steel of the chassis, voices erupted from inside. Sobs and curses sounded alike, muted by the container.

"Ayuda!" cried a young woman's voice. "Ayuda! Por favor!"

All hesitation left Lizzy. She reached the back of the container. The gate was locked; a thick padlock tied to some chains barred any entry. Lizzy shifted her camera around to her back. With her hands free, she pulled loose the hairpin she never used properly. It was more useful as a tool than a simple decoration.

Lizzy jammed the pin into the lock. Sweat pooled against her palms. Mentally ticking off the seconds between patrols, Lizzy sighed in relief when the padlock fell open and the chains slipped to the ground.

She lifted the gate to see the occupants inside. The metal squeaked from the strain, and a soft prayer slipped from her lips that the guards would not hear the movement. Dozens of men, women, and children filled the space. They were gaunt from malnourishment. Bruises decorated their arms and legs in various shades. Some hid their eyes from her, no longer used to any light, even the dim moonlight of the desert.

Lizzy held out her hand. "Estoy aqui para ayudarte."

None moved for her. She waved them on, her efforts interrupted by twin beams of light.

Company arrived in the form of a dozen men. Most remained in shadow, while the light from the flashlights almost blinded Lizzy. One stood taller than the rest. He wore a black bandanna, and snake tattoos adorned his arms that trailed down to his fingertips.

She recognized him from her research: Manny Guerra. He was well known in trafficking circles to be as slippery as the creatures who decorated his flesh. There were quite a few outstanding warrants for the man's arrest. Finding him, though, was the tricky part. He called nowhere home and held no human possessions. His work was all that mattered to him. In that regard, Lizzy understood the man.

"Looking for help?" Manny asked. His eyes were pinpricks in the dark, yet they appeared ravenous. "We'd be happy to lend you a hand."

A light dropped. The man holding the flashlight reached out for Lizzy. With his arm extended, Lizzy grabbed the man's wrist and snapped it back. He cried out in pain, but she held tight. Leaning forward with her left fist, Lizzy punched the bastard against the bridge of his nose. At the moment of impact, she let go of the man's wrist, and he fell to the dirt.

"My, oh my," Manny said. "We have a fighter here. I like that."

More hands shot out. Lizzy swatted at them, backpedaling to stay out of their reach. One leaped at her. His arms shot out, and his palms slammed into her chest. Lizzy twisted to her side as she fell. Rock dug into her arm from the impact. It was the least of her worries. She spun her camera away from the ground and held it tight.

As she stood, Manny stepped forward. His boys understood the gesture and retreated behind their leader. Manny reached out for her. She batted the hand away. His other hand shot out. When she moved to intercept, Manny grabbed her wrist and pulled her close.

"See? Two can play at that game," he said. She could smell the onions on his breath, and feel the heat rising from his chest. His yellow, twisted smile filled her view. "What do you say, boys? Should I add her to my collection?"

They cheered as one. They held no human decency and felt nothing for their fellow man. All that mattered to them was the promise of cold, hard cash to gamble or piss away on booze. This was their life. There was no desire for a future. They weren't building for their retirement. There was just the hope for a big payday at the expense of the innocent.

The cheers faded at the rise of another sound. All threw a questioning look at Manny, who mirrored their reaction. They were confused by the sound of laughter coming from Lizzy.

"What?" Manny shook at the girl in his grasp. "What's so funny?"

"'Add her to my collection?'" Lizzy asked. "I was going to say the same thing."

With her free hand, Lizzy lifted her camera in front of Manny's eyes. She snapped a photo. He reeled at the bright light, the flash temporarily blinding him. The moment his grip slackened along her wrist, Lizzy pulled free. She shoved Manny and raced for her freedom.

"Grab her!" Manny shouted.

The men gave chase. Shots rang out. They split the air around Lizzy. She cut sharply along the front of the trucks to the far side of the complex.

Cocking her head for a quick peek at her pursuers, she noticed Manny in the middle of the pack. Every last one had joined the chase. Her smile grew, and her pace quickened.

At the gas station, Lizzy ducked between the pumps. No more shots followed. The shouts of Manny and the others silenced their weapons. From the safety of the pumps, she proceeded to another group of trucks on the opposite side. Hands closed in on her. Her pursuers were everywhere. They moved faster, and more desperately, with each passing moment.

Lizzy fought ahead. Rounding the back of the trucks, she slid into the dirt. Manny and his crew scurried in pursuit. Each skidded to a halt at the sight before them.

Dozens of officers took aim at the criminals. In the center, wearing a wide-brim hat, was Sheriff Hector Ortega.

"Lower your weapons!" the sheriff yelled. "Then put your hands in the air!"

Manny shifted forward. He reached for Lizzy, who backed away for the line of cops. A single shot split the silence of the night. Manny glanced up to see a wisp of smoke rising from the barrel of Hector's gun.

"Not. Another. Step."

Manny grimaced, his balled-up fists slowly opening. He raised his hands into the air to surrender.

Lizzy lifted her camera to snap another photo.

Hector threw her an ice pack. Lizzy caught it with her left hand, then placed the pack along her right arm. Relief immediately spread in waves throughout her body.

She knew the pain would last a few days. She didn't care. Just the sight of Manny in the back of a police cruiser, and the dozens rescued from the twin trucks, was enough to make her forget about her injuries. Her actions saved lives, not that Hector would ever agree.

"You're an idiot, Doyle," he said. He joined her near the front entrance of the complex.

"Is that any way to thank me?"

Hector's hands fell on his hips. He was a cop through and through. There was no getting him to play a different tune — especially with her. "You're lucky I can talk to you, let alone thank you. They would have killed you, probably done worse for what you did to their leader."

"He had it coming."

"I told you we would handle this," Hector said. He always said the same thing. When she'd received the message from her contact about the transfer, Lizzy had passed it along to Hector.

Sure, she should have done that the second it came into her in-box and not two hours before she'd infiltrated the truck depot, but where was the fun in that?

Lizzy lifted her camera and took a picture of Hector's grimace. It was not appreciated. "You got your collar, Hector."

"And you got to appease your death wish for the day," Hector snapped back at her. "What about tomorrow, Lizzy?"

She rolled her eyes at the accusation. Coming home was a common practice for her. She tried to make the trip at least once every other month. There were bills to pay, and plants that needed to be replaced due to neglect.

It wasn't her fault work always crept up during her visits.

"Can we skip the speech this time?"

"Not a chance," he said. She turned from him. His hand settled on hers to hold her back. "Until you actually listen, I'm going to say it again and again. What you did here? It doesn't change what happened."

"It might, and you know it."

Frustration filled the sheriff's face. "Patrick's gone. He wouldn't have wanted this life for you."

Lizzy ripped her hand away from him. "Yeah, well, I'll be sure to ask him when I find him."

She made a beeline across the dirt road. Patrol cars exited the complex, causing her to stop and wait for the road to clear before she crossed. Hector followed close, but she refused to look in his direction. Instead, she focused on the shadow looming on the other side of the well-worn path.

The passenger van carried more rust than paint in certain areas. The blacked-out windows kept the contents within safe from any onlookers, and the vanity plates that read PHOTO1 always brought a smile to her face. It was her home, the piece of herself she always carried wherever she went. Unfortunately, it was another part of her life Hector failed to understand.

"How is this thing still running?"

"Duct tape and prayer," Lizzy replied. She headed for the driver's-side door. It creaked under her hand; the hinges threatened to snap loose from the body of the van. "I get your concern, Hector. I do, but—"

Her phone chirped in her pocket. Without a glance at her colleague, Lizzy dropped her camera into the van and pulled out the phone.

"Every time I hear that thing go off, I worry I won't see you again."

She read the name listed on the incoming notification, then tucked the device away. "I have to go."

Hector reached for her once more as she climbed inside the van. "Who is it this time? Who do you have to find?"

Lizzy tossed him the ice pack. Settling into her seat, she tried to get comfortable, though the padding had long since been worn out. The key turned in the ignition, and the engine struggled to turn over before roaring to life.

"A woman," she called out to her friend. "Someone named Emily Wright."

CHAPTER TWO

"You sure this is the right address?"

The place sat in the middle of a block filled with dilapidated townhouses. They butted against each other, the colorful sheen of decades past lost to weather and neglect. Few held any lights inside, but even from the street, voices could be heard within the vast majority. Be it television or domestic disputes, the neighborhood in downtown Wichita went on living without noticing the empty space in the center — a void left along the block.

Ben Riley opened the door to the abandoned unit; the wood barely hung on the frame. "Adler triangulated the call after it came through. This is the place."

The call had come late the previous night. Ben had been digging through more of Wesley Fuller's case files. After his recent discovery about the Witness, they had been his only focus. Something about the stories locked within had set off his imagination. Ben saw more in the reports, connections to bigger things. He knew they were the key to figuring out the Trust, the secret organization bent on controlling the world and everyone's fate.

The call had come through a landline. Adler explained it had been pulled from the DSA — a hotline left over from their former operational status. While the call had been mysterious, the caller was well known to Ben.

"I... n... hel...," the garbled voice said through the line. Static dominated the connection, yet the words had become clear with a little assistance from Nixon Jessup.

"I need your help, Ben."

The voice belonged to a missing woman, one Ben had been

searching for during every spare moment in his much-too-busy life. It was a voice he had listened to every night while on patrol in his former life, one that had filled the silence with laughter and joy.

Emily Wright's voice.

"This is it, Morgan," Ben said, holding the door open for his partner.

Morgan led the way through the townhouse, her Glock at her side. Ben pulled out a small flashlight from his pocket and followed.

Cobwebs filled the corners. Dust covered the broken remnants of furniture, from the decorative table in the hall to the chairs in the kitchen. Moonlight shone in through the cracked and torn blinds, lighting a path through the back half of the first floor.

"There's no one here, Ben," Morgan said. "There hasn't been anyone here in a long time."

Ben did his best to ignore her words. Frantic steps carried him through the living room. The carpet was stained throughout, like a pack of dogs had taken residence in the place for a spell just to finish what time and decay had started. The couch cushions were ripped open, the television screen smashed.

"Ben?"

He pushed through the webs strewn across the stairs. Ben's steps carried him up to the second floor. The wood creaked under his weight, the sound booming in the silence of the abandoned property. He entered a narrow hall where a pair of bedrooms branched off both sides. The room on the left was devoid of furniture and sat in shadow. Ben searched the space quickly, checking the closet for any clue, only to find more emptiness.

The room on the right was only slightly better. A lone item sat in the center of the floor: a phone. Ben carefully slipped on a glove. Crouching beside the object, Ben lifted the receiver. A dial tone rang out, the connection still active despite the vacant nature of the home.

He set the receiver back down, then joined it along the dust-laden floor. The glove snapped loose from his hand, and he tossed it across the space. It slapped the wall before falling to its final resting place.

"There's no one here, Ben."

He looked up to see his partner in the doorway. Sadness filled her words, her eyes mired in pity for the disappointed agent.

"I know," he muttered. He ran his hands through his hair in frustration. He was so sure this time. Every sign pointed to Emily being here. Yet, there was nothing.

Morgan took a slow step into the room. She kept to the fringes, lost to the darkness of the space. "What else did she say on the phone?"

"You heard the call, Morgan."

A slight nod escaped her. "Was there anything else during the call, something Nixon was able to glean, that might help us locate her?"

There wasn't. Nixon had had enough trouble pulling the voice through the static on the line. Again, Morgan knew as much as he did about the situation.

"Ben?" Morgan pressed. "If she isn't here, where would she be? Why bring us this far only to leave us in the dark? There has to be—"

"I don't know!" Ben snapped. "How the hell would I know?"

"I didn't mean to upset you." Morgan kept her voice low and calm, yet in each word, Ben sensed nothing but her doubts.

"I know exactly what you meant," Ben replied. "You don't think it was her on the line."

"Nixon couldn't verify—"

"I heard her voice, Morgan!" Ben shouted. Morgan staggered back a step, her hand raised in defense. Ben took a sharp breath to calm down. "I heard her voice. It wasn't imaginary or some delusion of hope. It was her. There was just too much static on the line. A bad connection or—"

"Or it was intentional."

Morgan had spent most of the trip questioning their visit. Finding nothing waiting for them cemented her feelings and drove daggers through Ben's skin.

"You don't have to be here," he said to his partner. He pushed past her for the hall and the stairs to the first floor. "I can handle this on my own."

She followed at his heels. "I'm not trying to diminish the one lead we've managed to grab, Ben. I want to help. I made that promise and I mean to keep it."

Ben settled at the base of the stairs. Her hand rested on his shoulder, a supportive squeeze offered to make him aware of her continued presence.

She was right. The promise had been made in the aftermath of their visit to Buffalo to solve a case. Morgan had no idea about Ben's relationship with his former partner. He had accused her of so much, but through it all, Morgan had stood by his side. In the end, she'd promised to do all she could to help in the search for Emily.

"I appreciate it."

"But--"

Ben tossed his hands in the air. "And then she ruined the moment."

"Come on, Ben," Morgan said. "Don't play it like that. There's a chance she was never here. That the call was bounced from somewhere else. That the call wasn't her. Just a jumble of signals passing through the ether."

Ben shook his head, unwilling to hear her theories. "So either it was Emily, or what? The ghost of my former partner? I refuse to accept that, Morgan. She's here. I can feel it."

Morgan's mouth opened with another argument ready. She held it back. Instead, she moved for the front door to the abandoned townhouse.

"Then let's canvass the area," she said. "Knock on some doors and see what the neighbors might have seen or heard."

Ben watched her depart for the street. He took one last look around the place. The emptiness caused his shoulders to slump and the weight of his mission to bear down on him.

His hope faded. Emily deserved better than him. Before his exile, they had had so much potential, so much love in their hearts. Neither had put their feelings into words before, out of respect for their work, or some needless professionalism that never cared one way or another for what went on during their private time.

The truth was that Ben had left too much unsaid. He needed to find Emily and make things right.

Ben stepped out of the home and shut the door behind him. He joined his waiting partner at the street. "Thanks for this, Morgan."

"I've got your back, partner," she said with a smile. They started for the closest home. "However long it takes. We'll find her."

CHAPTER THREE

Kanigher was bored. He'd spent the morning going through his usual routine. He had jogged the interior corridors of the Bunker, making sure to get his five miles in before heading to the workout room. There he'd welcomed a sparring match with the robotic dummies designed to simulate on-site crises. Nixon had devised them during his so-called spare time over the last week. A work in progress, he had called them. Kanigher had not cared one way or the other. He'd just wanted something to hit.

The Bunker was suffocating to him. The downtime between missions was even worse. Still, he'd tried to fill his day and get into a normal rhythm. The desire for a routine was for his own sanity, and also to allow him a chance to build a connection with the team.

To Morgan and Ben, Kanigher was nothing more than an outsider—an invader on their turf. They did not know how long he'd been working with Metcalf, nor the effort he had gone through to keep the DSA safe from Stallworth's interference. He realized it would take time to win them over.

From the training room, Kanigher had cleaned his service weapon twice over, then hit the showers. The quiet irritated him. The silence of the Bunker, the lack of stimulation from the outside world, gave him a headache.

Cooking had become Kanigher's passion. It had been something he'd dabbled in after his time in the military. There had always been something soothing about the process—like a balm on his troubled mind. Time, however, never measured out enough to allow him to really delve into the finer details of the act. Since joining the DSA, and removing himself from the natural order of the world, time seemed to grow in abundance.

No one commented on this new endeavor. Few mentioned the meals that made their way into the fridge for late-night binges. There were no words of thanks, and none were expected. Kanigher simply enjoyed cooking.

Despite the early hour, Kanigher looked to the kitchen for his latest project. He'd found a risotto recipe online to try out. He hoped Metcalf might want to join him in the adventure. That thought alone carried him from his shower to the main operation floor, and the sound of anger in the form of Alison Adler.

"No!" Her fingers slammed on the keyboard. She sat hunched over the terminal in the monitor womb. Twin displays shouted error messages in front of her. "No, no, no!"

"Adler?" Kanigher's steps were slow in approaching. He barely knew the woman, their few conversations pleasant, though he thought her to be too focused on other topics than the conversation at hand. Looking around to see if someone else wanted to handle Adler's tantrum, Kanigher found the place to be empty. "Adler, what is it?"

She pushed away from the screen and nearly took the keyboard with her. It slipped from her grasp and slammed along the desk. "I lost it again."

Kanigher said nothing. His steps clanged down the metal stairs to the monitor womb. He rounded the conference room table and joined her at the station.

Adler ran her hands over her face. A brief burst of anger screamed out before she let her hands fall away. Bags sat under her eyes. The steady stream of coffee obviously no longer cut it for her.

"Sorry."

"Don't be," Kanigher said. He peered at the screens. "What is it?"

Adler's chair slid back into position. "I thought I tracked the source of that rogue signal. The trace I've been running locked on for a full minute, and then poof. How could it disappear?"

The data looked like scribbles to Kanigher. He never claimed to be the most technically minded agent in the field or in the office. He was lucky his phone made calls when necessary, which was pretty much the extent of the technology he used on a daily basis.

"I thought Nixon was helping you with this?"

"Metcalf pulled him for something," she replied without looking. Her fingers returned to their work. So did the majority of her focus. "Neither said much about it. Or I wasn't listening, which is just as likely."

"I doubt it was you," Kanigher said. He ran his hand along his chin. Metcalf continued to play her games, even after their arguments over the tactics she'd used to recruit Nixon Jessup. There were supposed to be no more secrets. The DSA's success hinged on her ability to share, on leading the team, and not going it alone.

Of course, she wasn't alone this time. Nixon was with her. That made Kanigher more uneasy. Nixon wasn't a field agent. He wasn't even a proper analyst. His innate talent came from the other side of the law, and that worried Kanigher.

"Look," he said. "You're tired. Why not grab some shut-eye?"

"Can't," she answered, the word sharp. "Too much to do."

Kanigher sidled against the workstation, interrupting her typing. "I thought you said the signal disappeared."

"It did."

"Then what—" His question trailed off when he saw a familiar face fill one of Adler's screens. "Is that Modine?"

"It is."

Zac Modine was the former Head of Operations Support and Research for the DSA. When Sullivan had made his move to take over the department, Zac had stood by him. He had made a choice—the wrong one.

"You're tracking Zac?"

"I was," Adler said with a huff. She turned away from the monitor and rubbed her eyes. "I lost him in Connecticut. He bought a ticket for Bethesda, but never boarded the bus. I thought he might be coming home."

"Why?"

"I wish I knew."

"No," Kanigher said. "I mean, why are you looking for him? After what he did?"

"He made a mistake," Adler said. "We've all done that, haven't we?"

Kanigher offered no reply. Part of him wondered if this was

his bad choice: supporting the DSA over his allegiance to his country. He had taken an oath, both with his military career and his time at the NSA. Had he tossed away everything he'd believed in by joining Metcalf?

"I think he's paid enough," Adler said. She shifted back to the screens. "He deserves to come home."

Kanigher bit back his first reaction. Zac did more than choose Sullivan. He had acted to sabotage Metcalf's authority on more than one occasion. People had died because of him. Still, Kanigher let it rest.

"So you're running a program to root him out?" Kanigher stared at the commands Adler punched in at lightning speed. "Looks complicated."

Adler nodded. "I inputted a series of queries. Each targeted one of Zac's usual habits. Manner of dress, takeout orders, old logins and passwords. So far, nothing."

A small blip lit up on Alder's second screen. She was too busy typing to notice. Kanigher pointed to the blip. "What's that, then?"

"Hmm?" she asked. Her fingers left the keys. She followed his finger to the second monitor, and her eyes widened in surprise. "Oh!"

She clicked on the icon. A window opened up and displayed Zac near a payphone outside what appeared to be a diner.

"You found him."

Adler smiled. "Arcadia, Missouri."

"See, Adler? All that work—"

"Meant nothing," she said. She shook her head and pointed to the phone in the image. "My searches weren't what triggered the trace. I've also been tapping his wife's phone. He just called her from that location."

Adler pushed away from the desk. She was on her feet and at the stairs before Kanigher could blink.

"Hey," he called after her. "Where are you going?"

Adler's brow furrowed. "Arcadia, Missouri. I thought that was obvious."

"On your own?"

"He deserves another chance, Kanigher. Feel free to join me."

"But…" Kanigher glanced at the kitchen. His risotto called to him. So did Adler's mission. He sighed. The risotto would have to wait. "Fine. I walked into this. I may as well see it through."

CHAPTER FOUR

"You can't keep avoiding me."

Zac heard the words in the back of his mind. They trailed his every thought, winding through the myriad pathways of his brain, like a never-ending film on repeat. They echoed in the emptiness of the night and screamed in the rush of the day. If it came down to it, he would avoid them for the rest of his life, just as he had for the last week.

The words continued to play in the background as he finished his hike. The Ozark Trail offered him a reprieve from the world, and the wilderness dimmed the voice in the back of his mind. Hiking had never been his style before. Physical activity always impeded actual work. That might have accounted for his weight problem, and the habitual need for a snack break every hour on the hour.

Since his arrival to Arcadia, hiking had become Zac's only break from the world. Through the twists and turns of the trails, Zac found himself at peace. Today's eight-mile endeavor was no different. Sweat poured down his face. It soaked his shirt, now two sizes too large for him. He hadn't taken to the scale since leaving Connecticut, but his weight loss had not abated. A lack of appetite contributed, his inability to keep anything other than trail mix down another factor. No more fast food. No more drinking coffee by the pot. Everything was water and nuts.

God, he hated it.

That was true about everything for Zac. He even hated the hike, of hiding instead of facing things head on. Yet every time the voice returned, his first instinct was to hide, flee, and cower before the unknown danger rather than to learn more about it.

Rather than solving the problem, Zac had ignored it.

"Did you hear me?" the voice said. "You can't keep avoiding me."

He knew that much to be true. He had tried back in Connecticut. The bus ticket for Bethesda had been in hand, and its departure imminent. The voice had kept him from getting aboard. Zac had fought against the pull, and lost consciousness. When light returned to his world, Zac had found himself in Missouri.

The blackouts were getting more frequent. The time stolen from his life became more extensive, from minutes to hours, and sometimes even whole days slipped away without warning.

Still, Zac tried to avoid the voice. The woods made it possible. Away from the hum of electronics and the bustle of humanity, the Ozark Trail afforded Zac his own precious time. Zac used it in an effort to come up with a solution to the innate problem hidden in his head. None presented—not a single answer to the unending questions over what was happening to him.

The hikes only delayed the inevitable. They only sped up his anxiety when they ended and nothing was solved.

Today was no different. Zac left the woods behind, yet stopped short of the road. It was another mile to his hotel room, but he settled on a neighborhood bench to rest. Water soothed him, the bottle empty in seconds. Some joined his clinging shirt, the fabric completely saturated.

He stared out at the morning sun. There was beauty in the glowing light, something he'd never appreciated before. Work had ruled his life. The last month, first in Connecticut and then Missouri, showed him a different side to the world. He witnessed quiet moments of humanity where work never infringed on living. For Zac, work was all there ever was, and his dedication continued to cost him dearly.

A sudden sensation sent Zac away from the bench for the adjacent rest stop. He scrambled across the parking lot to the restroom. The door slammed open in his haste, then crashed back into the frame. His chest heaved, his anxiety threatening to spill out as easily as the contents in his stomach. His hands clasped tight to the side of the sink. He stared at himself in the dusty and stained mirror. His pale eyes begged for help, for a chance to keep it all together and not fall apart.

Unfortunately, his eyes failed to provide the response. "I told you. You can't avoid me forever."

April Newton stared back. The elderly woman's visage took over his own in the reflection; her knowing smile grated the overwhelmed former analyst.

His hands ripped from the sink. His head spun away from the mirror. "I can sure as hell try."

"And how is that working out for you?" she called after him.

He stopped moving. His feet refused to take another step. His hand shot out for the handle to the door, only to stop an inch away from the metal. The hand fell limply to his side, suddenly impotent to act.

"Let go of me!" Zac shouted. "I'll fight you!"

"You can, Zachary," April said in a motherly tone. "But it will be unpleasant."

His hands slammed against his temples. Pain wracked his head. It shot down his arms, then down his legs, and he fell to the floor. Curled up against the cold, disgusting concrete, Zac screamed.

She was doing this to him. April was in his mind, the voice at the heart of everything he had been running from for so long, and she refused to give up her hold on him.

"All right!" he said. "All right!"

The pain subsided. Slowly, motor function returned and Zac found his way back to his feet. He staggered to the sink. Drool ran from his lips, and he swiped at it.

April watched over him, her presence filling the mirror. "Wonderful," she said. "It's about time we had that little chat, don't you think?"

CHAPTER FIVE

Lizzy snapped another photo. She carried her Nikon with the telephoto lens to give her some distance. The view, however, kept her right in the thick of things. It was her go-to weapon in a fight. Nothing stood up to a captured image, not when seen in all its megapixel glory.

She'd arrived in Wichita just prior to sundown. Upon entering the city limits, Lizzy had found a quiet place to park. The drive had been longer than she'd thought, and her bones ached from sitting against the less than comfortable cushion for so long. Hopping into the back of the van, she'd caught a couple hours of sleep before getting back to work.

It hadn't taken long to track the location of Emily Wright's recent call. Why it had been scrambled through multiple lines remained a mystery to Lizzy. If Emily had been reaching out for help, why in such a scattered way? Why call at all instead of heading to the local police department for help? The questions continued to add up when Lizzy arrived.

That was when she found the pair of so-called agents already on the scene. Their behavior reeked of law enforcement, from the way they held their heads high to the way they flashed their badges at every neighbor along the block. The badges, however, gave her pause. She had seen plenty of forgeries over her short career; she'd even fallen for a few of the best ones. These weren't even close, yet the occupants of the block never questioned them.

The second red flag was the lack of local support. Canvassing a neighborhood took resources. These two didn't have a single beat cop assisting them. That meant they weren't authorized.

They held no jurisdiction on the case.

Not that there really was much of a case to begin with. Neighbors in Buffalo had made reports of an incident at the Wright home, and had been concerned about Emily, yet there had been no follow-up by local PD. The matter had fallen through the cracks by the time Lizzy became aware of the missing woman.

Lizzy had only stumbled upon it thanks to her network of contacts. Each supplied intel through others, which fed into databases she had tapped into. Few leads were obtained legally. Her constant movement, and her usually subtle methods of investigation, helped keep her off the radar of major law enforcement.

Checking the recent image, Lizzy's brow furrowed. The pair was unusual. They argued and joked, almost at the same time in some instances. Their professionalism needed work, but they continued to head down the row of townhouses for some clue to Emily's whereabouts.

Lizzy returned to the viewfinder. She trailed them along the sidewalk, trying to read each question asked. An older woman in her bathrobe dismissed them from her stoop. Undeterred, the pair of agents moved to the next stoop for another round of questions. When the door slammed in their face, the pair shifted to the bottom step of the stoop and sat.

The gentleman with the brown hair and dusty eyes appeared distraught. The lack of answers from the neighbors definitely disturbed him. His partner stuck close to his side. Her hand settled on his knee, and she squeezed to coax some life out of him.

Lizzy lowered her camera for a second. The man's reaction surprised her. She had seen investigators handle missing person's cases before—and by handle she meant coast along with little to no intent, and no emotional connection. This pair was different. They seemed genuinely concerned for Emily's well-being and her safety.

As she settled in for another shot, Lizzy noticed the red light blinking on her camera. The battery demanded attention, and she quietly cursed her lack of preparation. She typically had everything charged and ready to go. The long drive had thrown her off schedule.

Leaving the safety of her position, Lizzy made her way to her van. It was parked around the corner, away from her subjects, yet close enough to reach if there was any trouble. Quickly, Lizzy rounded the vehicle and opened the passenger-side door. She dug through her bags for her backup battery pack—one of six she traveled with. Swapping the dying battery for the fresh one, Lizzy made sure her camera was set before heading back. She nestled along the brick of the corner store and raised the camera into position.

Her subjects were gone. The two agents no longer sat on the stoop. Using the camera, Lizzy scanned the rest of the block for signs of the pair, only to see the vacant street.

"Where the hell did they go?" she muttered. Lizzy lowered the camera to her side and stepped out from the brick wall shielding her presence. She looked up and down the block for signs of life, and found none. "Gave up already? No surprise there."

Lizzy returned to the van. She wanted to make sure her equipment was set so she could check out the exact location of Emily's recent call. Everything appeared ready to go in the back of the van. All she needed to do was move into position. Closing the back door, Lizzy turned and nearly bowled into a man wearing a bloodstained tie.

"Excuse me," the man said. A wry smile spread across his face. It was the agent from the stoop.

"My fault," Lizzy said. She spun on her heels and circled the van for the driver's-side door. The other agent was waiting for her, badge on full display.

"We have some questions for you."

"Funny," Lizzy replied. "I was about to say the same thing."

CHAPTER SIX

Her feet pounded with each stride. She kept her eyes toward the ground, the pavement cracked and uneven in spots. Heart pumping in tune with her legs, Miriam Prescott jogged along the outskirts of Newman University.

It was her one escape. When everything started to weigh down on her, Miriam loved to strap on her sneakers and head out to the wooded area on the edge of campus. No one ever occupied the path—not on foot, anyway. An access road met up with the larger dorms to the south of the quad, but traffic remained sparse. For most of her visits, it was just her and her thoughts in a never-ending battle.

Things were not well. She recognized it with her quickening pace and her heavier than normal breathing. Her parents were fighting again. They always thought their marital problems were well hidden, but Miriam recognized the tension on the phone when she'd checked in earlier.

It came down to the same issues: her dad's constant work, her mother's smoking. Nothing was ever resolved between them. Talking about their problems always turned to arguing, so silence typically masked everything in her household. The damn tension in the room during her breaks from school had made Miriam want to scream.

As if her home life wasn't enough, now problems cropped up with her boyfriend as well. He wanted more attention, not caring about the upcoming midterms or the stress of her parent's failing marriage. Jim was nothing but a self-centered child, but they had been together for so long she'd grown accustomed to his weekly tantrums. It was another gift learned from her parents, and she cursed her inability to break up with the man-child and move on with her life.

She felt powerless over everything. Her world needed her, pulled at her to act on behalf of everyone else at all times, without offering a single reprieve for herself. There was never a girls' night out, or a day to bum around and watch crappy rom-coms while pigging out on stale popcorn.

Her roommates didn't understand. Their lives were perfect, no struggles with school and no relationship issues. Sure, they asked about her. They were concerned about the pressure she put on herself and offered to help where they could. She never asked, never spoke up. It wasn't her nature. She merely suffered quietly through it all.

School was the same way. Her grades continued to slip, another effect of everything else weighing down on her. She lacked direction. Nothing spoke to her as a career, and she worried nothing ever would.

Miriam grunted in frustration. The jog offered no reprieve. Her thoughts pounded against her skull worse than her feet on the pavement. She slowed to catch her breath, turning the run into a walk. The change in pace knocked one of her ear buds loose.

"Crap," she muttered. The small device fell to the ground. Bending low, Miriam snatched at the rolling piece of tech. She caught the speaker at the edge of the path. As she slipped it back in her ear, she paused. Steps continued to patter against the ground despite the pause in her walk.

Miriam glanced at the periphery, afraid to turn around completely. There was a truck parked just off the access road, the back hidden behind the brush. She had passed the shadowed vehicle without noticing.

"Oh, God," she whispered. Miriam ripped the headphone from her other ear and tucked both in her pocket. She kept walking at a brisk pace. The main entrance to the campus was still a mile away, the road back to her room twice that distance. She refused to look behind her, afraid to trip along the uneven sidewalk.

The footsteps continued to approach. Miriam started to run, but it was too late. A hand snatched her right arm. With a firm grip, the hand — definitely a man's from the size and strength —

pushed her toward the woods to the left.

"No!" Miriam cried as she fell into the brush. Twisted brambles dug into her, cutting along exposed arms and legs.

A shadow grew over her. The figure's heavy breathing and grunting caused her to panic. His hand reached for her again, and Miriam kicked out at his chest.

"Get away from me!"

He said nothing. His hands snatched her flailing feet, then knocked her legs aside to avoid her frantic blows. He pinned them away with his left hand, while his right fist shot out before she could defend herself. It connected with her cheek and slammed her back into the woods. Branches scraped her face, and blood dripped from her forehead down over her eye.

"Please," she begged. Her voice wasn't strong, the word lost to the man's excitement. Nothing about her was strong enough to protect herself.

Another blow rained down on her, then another, until she couldn't see anything but darkness.

CHAPTER SEVEN

Flashbulbs threatened to blind him the moment he stepped from the back seat of the limousine. Questions flew from the press gathered around the rope line. They ranged from allegations of substandard materials used in his latest product launch to what was being served during the third course for his guests.

Sebastian Duloc smiled at each and every one. He took their questions in stride, offering the manufactured claptrap as his response. Each answer was canned and aged to perfection, all to disarm the already limp-wristed members of the media. They craved a story, but more than anything, they demanded attention. The more attention, the better their ratings, and the more they could control the narrative.

Sebastian knew the game very well. He had perfected it by the time he made his first million at the age of twenty. Now well into his forties, the game was nothing but a bore—a tired rendition of the same cues—yet he continued to play his part.

As one of the foremost businessmen in digital technologies, Sebastian oversaw more in one day than most people could imagine in a lifetime. There were cell phones, of course; Sebastian owned one of the premier manufacturers and distributed more units around the globe than even those other guys with the fruit as their logo.

Duloc was synonymous with the future in most eyes, so he weaponized that look for the public. From the parties to the boardroom, Sebastian used each opportunity to further the brand.

The public ate it up.

They weren't the only ones. There were also the sycophants

and the well-wishers, always wanting a piece of the pie. Stockholders and lobbyists pushed their agenda with the same amount of flair. They sought to bend his ear. This party was for them to an extent—at least the public side of events.

The doors opened to the lobby. Sebastian entered to another array of flashbulbs and praise. Guests swarmed at his arrival. Employees from the London branch of Duloc Technologies mingled beside stockholders from Taiwan, Munich, and a dozen other cities around the globe. Every guest carried some form of technology developed by Sebastian's conglomerate: phones, compacts, beepers, and more. His company developed them all, and now he owned every single person in the room.

"Sebastian!" a woman bellowed from the base of the lobby steps. Sebastian made his way deeper into the room. The woman shoved through the crowd. Sebastian hid the wince of his eyes behind a smile. Rebecca Giroux owned half the fashion industry thanks to her insipid reviews on national television. She was a bitter woman who thrived on capitulation from both sexes in her presence. "I didn't think you were coming."

"And miss my own party?" Sebastian answered with an air of drama. He leaned forward and kissed the back of the woman's hand. "Never."

"I was concerned," Rebecca said.

"You should never be concerned," Sebastian replied. "Enjoy the party."

"But—"

"Excuse me. I'm looking for someone." Sebastian moved on from the woman. Her cries were silenced by another approaching group. The couple stuck close together. They were Henrietta and Bradford Jones: Hollywood producers who financed three of the last four billion-dollar blockbusters. Those were the projects the public knew about. They never conceived of the ten other films produced to influence the minds of the world's youth—or that each featured Duloc Technologies in one form or another.

"Jones!" Sebastian shouted over the roar of the crowd. "I was glad you both could make it."

"Your proposal intrigued us, to say the least," Henrietta said.

"Then I think you will be most interested in the main festivities at the penthouse."

"Not down here?" Bradford asked. "Why the secrecy?"

"You'll see, my friend." Sebastian winked at the man and all laughed. "Head up when you can."

"We were worried you were a no show," Henrietta admitted with wide eyes.

Sebastian read the look clearly. His sneer threatened to envelop the woman. "I wouldn't miss this for the world."

Bradford cut between them with a chuckle. He passed a chute of champagne to their host. "Being fashionably late never goes out of style."

Sebastian held the glass up for a toast. "Like money and beautiful women."

Henrietta flushed at the comment. Then she glanced behind the man with curiosity. "No one on your arm tonight, Sebastian? How tragic."

"She's here." Sebastian looked around the crowd until settling on the object of his desire. "She came earlier to avoid the cameras. She tends to draw a crowd."

They turned to see her standing nearby. Deep brown eyes caught each of them. Her raven hair flowed over her shoulders. A ruby red, backless dress sparkled under the lights of the hotel lobby.

"Alexa," Sebastian said breathlessly.

She smiled at him, a hand out for him to kiss. "You're late."

Alexa had arrived an hour earlier and settled into the crowd. She'd tried to keep her presence muted, the dress unfortunately having the opposite effect. Still, she'd made the best of the time, noting each guest, especially the ones that had headed for the elevator and the penthouse above.

"Wow," Bradford mouthed. Henrietta caught her husband's stare and elbowed him in the gut lightly.

"You look radiant, my love." Sebastian pulled the woman close.

Alexa's smile refused to diminish, despite the man's probing fingers. "I like to look my best for you."

Sebastian's hungry eyes grew. Bradford cleared his throat to draw the host back to his party. Sebastian straightened his back, gaining a few inches on the beauty at his side. "Right. Alexa, this is Bradford and Henrietta Jones. They are here to help me change the world."

"A pleasure," Alexa said.

Bradford stepped closer, his hand extended for hers. "It's all mine."

Henrietta slapped his hand down. "He means ours."

Dots of sweat formed along her husband's brow. "Of course. Of course, that's what I meant."

"Sebastian," another man called. He cut between the Jones' for a better view of the pair. Reaching out, he shook Sebastian's hand. Disdain filled Sebastian's eyes. A shared glance with Bradford told the rest of the story. When Bradford made a motion toward the penthouse festivities with his finger, Sebastian shook his head. The newcomer to their group hadn't been invited to the true party.

It wasn't surprising, considering who the man was. Sebastian took his hand and gave a hard shake before letting it fall away. "Glad you could make it, Mr. Field."

Oliver Field was just another faceless mogul. He'd made his fortune on the stock market, but never went further with his ambitions. Field doled out millions during the last election cycle, always betting on the winner no matter the politics involved. He was an opportunist, not a participant in the true dealings of the night, and Sebastian treated him as such.

Still, Field persisted for his moment in the sun with their host. "You oughta be ashamed, hiding this treasure from us. Don't we give enough business to your tech firm?"

Sebastian's icy stare gave the answer, but he rolled with the joke and replied with a disarming grin. "Never enough business, my friend. But you can make up for it by booking a suite or three."

"Wait," Field said with surprise. "The hotel is one of yours?"

"Tonight, everything is mine."

He leaned over and kissed Alexa deeply. She held onto the kiss, and the entire world faded for a long moment. When he relented, she continued to hold tight to his tie.

"I should think so," she said with a whisper in his ear. "The sooner, the better."

"My dear, I..." Alexa kissed him again. The force of her passion nearly sent them tumbling through a crowd of passing guests and into the foliage surrounding the fountain in the center of the lobby. Sebastian struggled to pull away, then turned to their staring friends. "Well, it was good to see you, Mr. Field."

"Of course." Field was still staring at Alexa. He appeared flush from the scene he'd just witnessed. Alexa's smile widened at his discomfort.

Sebastian pushed through Field, Alexa in tow, and leaned close to Bradford. "I hope to see you at the penthouse, my friend."

Bradford nodded. Henrietta agreed. "We wouldn't miss it."

"Excuse us, won't you?" Alexa took the lead, helping Sebastian through the crowd.

"Of course," Henrietta said.

"Lucky devil," Bradford muttered. His wife slapped his arm soundly.

Alexa led Sebastian away from the bustle of the lobby. Well-wishers trailed them, but they passed each with a knowing look from their host. The time for pleasantries was at an end for the moment. The main event was about to begin for Sebastian Duloc.

"Where are we heading, Alexa?"

"I was thinking..." She stopped before the bank of elevators. Her hand ran through Sebastian's shirt, then grabbed tight to his tie once more. She pulled him close, her lips upon his ear and her hot breath washing over him. "Somewhere private?"

She pressed the call button on the elevator. Sebastian turned back to the lobby. "What about our guests?"

Kisses ran up his neck. His legs quivered. "They don't need to see what comes next," Alexa said between kisses. "Unless you don't care to find out for yourself?"

The ding of the elevator rang out. Car doors opened and Alexa pulled Sebastian inside by his tie. A couple followed them for the elevator, but stopped short when they saw the pair already inside. The second the doors closed, Alexa let go of Sebastian's tie.

He straightened and attempted to regain his composure. "Oh, I do. Very much so. I've waited patiently since I met you."

"Yes, you have," Alexa said. Her fingers danced along his pants. "I should reward that patience."

A growl escaped Sebastian at her teasing. "Where?"

"The penthouse?"

"We can't," Sebastian said. "There are other rooms..."

"A simple bed?" Alexa frowned. Her hands worked over his back and kneaded his shoulders. "I think there are more exciting places for what I have in mind. Take me somewhere different, Sebastian. Drive me wild."

Sebastian fought to catch his breath. He reached into his pocket and removed a small golden key. Placing it in the control box for the elevator, a panel opened beneath the standard array of floors. A single button lit up with the label SUBBASEMENT on display.

"Anything for you, my love." He depressed the button, and the car shifted into gear.

The car headed down until it came to a halt. The doors opened. Instead of the opulence of the hotel, which ran in golden colors with warm lighting on the walls, they stepped out on cold tile and bright overhead lights.

"Welcome to my home away from home."

The space was open in the center, but corridors branched off in six directions. Medical equipment lined the right-hand wall. Shelving occupied the left side. It was filled with technical manuals and schematics. In the middle of the open space was a single display. It showed the model of a city. Beneath, a placard read UTOPIA PROTOCOL.

"This is a lab?" Alexa asked.

Sebastian nodded, proud of the room. "Next gen tech development. This is where we make advancements in medicine and a dozen other fields. All hidden under the hotel to keep the government off my back."

There might have been some truth in his words, but she read the lie just as easily. The hotel was most assuredly Sebastian's, but the lab went well beyond his talents. It screamed of a bigger organization.

"Such a sly man," she cooed in his ear. "Devilish. I like that."

She ripped open his shirt. Kissing his chest, the man struggled to stay upright. Sebastian leaned against the city model, letting her work her way down his body.

Shadows grew over them. Both stopped at the sight of two men approaching from the corridor on the far side of the room.

"Alexa," Sebastian said.

Alexa smiled innocently and stood away from the half-naked man. "How silly. I thought we were alone."

"You shouldn't be here, sir," one of the men said. "We're still completing our sweep."

Alexa pouted. Sebastian straightened up to meet the men at their level. "You can finish it later."

"Sir?"

"Now," Sebastian said with a deep glare.

The other man nodded. He pulled at his companion, and the pair started for the elevator. "You heard the boss."

The second the doors closed on them, Alexa picked up where she left off. She kissed him, forcing him back against the city model.

"Such power. Such force," she said. "I want you now."

"Yes," Sebastian answered. "Alexa—"

She stopped him, a finger over his lips. "I have such plans for you, my love. But first..."

Alexa opened her handbag and retrieved her lipstick.

"I don't think that's necessary, my dear."

"It definitely is." Alexa popped the cap. Instead of the ruby red to match her lips, the container revealed a syringe.

"What?" Sebastian said in dismay. He tried to move away from her, but she held him in place. "What are you—"

The needle jabbed him in the neck. Sebastian winced at the sting, then again, once Alexa hit the plunger on the small syringe. Sebastian floundered as the drug hit his system. He looked at her with hazy eyes, then collapsed to the ground.

Alexa circled him. Her heels clacked against the tile, as she waited for a sign her companion was unconscious. She kicked him in the gut for good measure. Sebastian was out, leaving her free rein in the subbasement.

She slipped out of her heels, then set the empty syringe into her handbag. Digging through the contents, Alexa removed a small earbud and slipped it in her right ear.

A voice filled her ear. "I don't know how much more I could have listened to," Nixon Jessup said. His disgust was clear.

Alexa understood completely. She ripped off the wig atop her head and let her auburn hair flow free once again. Her deep brown contacts gave way to stone blue eyes. Alexa was gone. Standing in her place was Susan Metcalf, a sigh of relief slipping from her lips as she wiped away any trace of Sebastian's kisses.

"Yeah, well, it worked." She looked around the secret lab and grinned. "I'm in."

CHAPTER EIGHT

Zac wiped the water from his eyes, then grabbed for the towel on the rack. Steam filled the room. The shower cleaned the stench from his body, but did little to take away his perpetual exhaustion. His body fought to stand upright, and his eyes struggled to stay open despite the early evening hour.

It didn't matter what he did, how long he slept, or how little he accomplished during the day, the evening hours always hit the hardest. Try as he might, nothing seemed to help.

Zac finished drying off. He slipped on his clothes and moved to the bathroom mirror. He ran his hand along the surface to clear the steam from the glass.

April waited for him behind the mist. "Feel better now?"

"Do you have to do that?" Zac straightened his shirt and tucked in the excess material.

"A little shy?"

"I happen to like my privacy," Zac said.

April's lip curled. "I'm in your head, Zachary. Privacy is a thing of the past. And besides, it's nothing I haven't seen before."

Zac closed his eyes. "Don't remind me."

He started for the door when April called him back. "You asked for time. I gave it to you."

"An hour," Zac said. "You gave me an hour to wrap my head around this so-called conversation."

"You know that isn't true, Zachary," April replied.

"Stop with the Zachary, like it's some sign of respect. For someone in my head, you should know how much I hate my whole name."

April offered a slight nod. "Apologies. Zac."

"Thank you."

"You do realize today's reprieve is the last delay in this matter," April continued. "You asked for a chance to groom yourself—not that it helped much, in my opinion—and now it is time to 'face the music' as they say."

"Face the music?" Zac asked in disbelief. He swung his arms in the air, then left the bathroom for the bedroom of his rented space. "That's all I've been doing!"

The bed was a mess, sheets in every direction from another troubled night of sleep. Despite his perpetual exhaustion, no relief came when Zac attempted to rest. In fact, the more he looked at the bed, the more his anxiety spiked. The same held true with every glance around the room.

One week ago, Zac had tried to head home to see his wife. His plan had been clear: save his marriage and beg for forgiveness from the one woman who ever really loved him. Claire was the only person who understood Zac. She recognized his foibles, his weaknesses, and loved him all the same. He'd thrown it all away out of desire, but he'd wanted to fix it and make things right.

Instead of reaching Bethesda by bus, Zac had woken up in the disheveled bed in Arcadia, Missouri. The plaque near the door had brought the destination fully into focus: The Academy Bed & Breakfast. A full day had passed like a blur, as Zac had tried to acclimate to his new surroundings. None had been his choice.

They had been April's.

He hated the room. A history lesson accompanied every picture on the wall. Every piece of furniture was uniform and drab.

"I like it here, Zac." April's image shifted from the bathroom to the dresser mirror.

Of course, she knew his thoughts on the room. She knew his thoughts on everything and had ever since their meeting at the Cove.

"Bully for you," Zac seethed. He collapsed on the side of the bed. His hands ran to his temples, the pain still present from their earlier argument. There was no avoiding the conversation any longer. He dropped his hands and turned to the mirror, unable to see himself in the glass. Only the woman locked in the back of his mind. "Care to explain why?"

"I bought this place centuries ago," April said. Her words were matter-of-fact. They did little to temper Zac's reaction.

"Centuries?" Zac asked, bounding from the bed. He shot toward the mirror, stopping short of the end of the dresser. "April Newton was only in her seventies."

"She was."

Zac read the look in her eyes. "You're not talking about April."

"I'm not April," she said. "You know that, don't you?"

"Not April?" Zac's hand returned to his cheek. April Newton had touched the same spot. Light had filled his entire being from her contact, and minutes had been lost. "You're not April. You're--"

"The Wellspring."

"A program."

"A protocol," April corrected. "One far older than you know."

"But I should," Zac snapped. "You're in my head. I should know everything."

"You're fighting it, Zac," she said. Eyes washed over him with concern. "And it's starting to show."

Zac pushed off the dresser. "So why here?"

"There were pleasant memories here," April said. "In 1848, I turned this place into one of the most prestigious schools in the country."

Zac shook his head and chuckled. "Feeding students knowledge to suit your needs."

"And theirs."

Zac shot her a disdainful look. "How magnanimous of you."

"You're angry."

"Why wouldn't I be?" Zac shouted. "I bought a bus ticket for home and woke up in Missouri. You used my body!"

"You refused to listen."

"To a voice in my head!" Zac's arms flailed in frustration.

Hushed murmurs carried beneath the door to his room. Footsteps rushed down the hall. He was causing a scene. That was all he appeared capable of doing lately.

"Zac," the voice called him back. "You must complete the process. You must accept the Wellspring Protocol."

Zac shook his head. "Not a chance."

"Resisting will kill you."

He felt like he was dying already. Losing time, first in minutes and now by days, Zac thought death would have been a welcome reprieve from the pain he'd experienced since departing the Cove.

"And if I do?" The thought took root in his mind and he wondered if it was his own, or if April—or whatever it was he was speaking to—had tired of the back and forth. It sickened him to see his life spinning so completely out of his own control. "If I accept this programming, your Wellspring Protocol, what happens to me then?"

No answer came. Silence filled the space. The eerie calm in their spat did nothing to settle Zac's nerves.

"Yeah, that's what I thought." Either way was a death sentence if April's silence was any indication. Continuing to resist the programming from latching to his mind would cause his body to fail. Accepting the protocol, however, would overwrite his personality. He would be one with the Wellspring—and Zac Modine no longer. "There has to be a way to stop it. There is, isn't there?"

"Zac..."

"Tell me!" Zac bellowed at the image in the mirror.

"The signal," April said.

Zac staggered back a step. The signal. Those two words decorated every wall of the Vroman's living room in Connecticut. They had been part of the scribblings of a madman, or so Zac imagined, having woken up in the middle of a fever dream. The two words were buried in lines of code, yet with every glance they spoke to their own importance when Zac thought about them. They meant something more—something vital to his survival.

"What is it?"

April sighed. "It feeds the knowledge to the Wellspring. Each of us, in turn, passes along the data provided by the signal to the public as needed."

The Wellspring was rumored to be the reason for humanity's advancement over the centuries. Every technological breakthrough, every medical advancement, and more were laid at the feet of this being. Yet the knowledge came from somewhere else.

"Why?"

Silence answered his question.

Frustration grew and Zac clenched his fists tight at his sides. "How can you hold back information from me? You're in my head!"

Zac grabbed his coat and moved for the door. Slamming the door shut behind him, he stopped to rest along the frame for a brief second. He needed something to drink, something to eat, despite the cramps in his gut and the fire in his head.

Starting for the exit to the former school, April's image followed in the mirrors that ran the length of the hall. "You can stop the signal," April said. "You can disrupt it and break the transmission. But you shouldn't."

Zac caught the worry in her voice and smirked. "Concern for me? Or for your own protocol?"

Eyes trailed Zac. Bystanders backed away when he approached. His mutterings brought discomfort to their faces. Even the staffers kept their distance or moved quickly in the opposite direction.

Zac left the milling crowds of the lobby for the breezeway. April's pale reflection caught on the outer door. "Tell me how," Zac said. "Or where. Tell me something!"

April said nothing. She merely shook her head, then vanished from view.

"April?" Zac called. He leaned closer to the glass. "Don't you dare disappear now!" A hand slapped at the cold reflection, his own tired eyes the only ones staring back at him. "Get back here!"

The door opened. Zac nearly tumbled out and down the front steps. A man stood in the open entryway, confusion on his face. "Was there some trouble with the door?"

Zac wiped his hands along his jeans. "No. No trouble at all."

The man shrugged and headed inside. Zac continued for the steps, but stopped short at the sight of two individuals waiting for him at the bottom.

"Great," he muttered.

"Zac?" Adler smiled at his approach. Kanigher grumbled, his arms across his chest. "It is you."

"What are you doing here, Adler?"

She pushed through the agitation in his voice. Her cheerful demeanor remained. "We should talk," she said. "How about a cup of coffee?"

CHAPTER NINE

There were better things to do with their time. Morgan's thought carried her from the abandoned townhouse on the outskirts of Wichita down the road to a country bar less than a mile from the local university. Their visit had been ill-advised and rushed because of Ben's impatience. Emily Wright was too important to her partner to ignore, despite the lack of evidence.

Still, Morgan had joined him. She had made the promise, and there had been no way to ignore the obligation. Ben's life had been ripped from him when he'd lost his position in Buffalo thanks to the Trust's involvement. In the process, or due to his role in the DSA—they still were not sure exactly—Emily had disappeared. Not just vanished, the former officer had been wiped from existence. Her colleagues at the precinct had no recollection of her working there, and her childhood home had been cleaned of her belongings.

That had been plenty of cause for concern with Ben. Morgan, however, had tried to keep him grounded. Missing person's cases were long haul affairs, sometimes taking years to solve. It was especially true considering the time that had passed since Emily had gone missing. It had been months without a single word, a thread or a lead to guide them, and now their search had brought them to Wichita... and, it seemed, to Lizzy Doyle.

While Morgan might have been reticent about the sudden trek to the Sunflower State, she was more wary about their newfound companion. Lizzy—even the name irritated Morgan—ensnared Ben's full attention. Her interest in Emily's disappearance immediately bonded them together.

His captivation with the woman caused him to jump at the

chance to take their conversation elsewhere. She had been the one to suggest the nearby drinking establishment. The line had been drawn when she'd offered to drive. Morgan, instead, had made sure to control that much of the situation, and had led the pair back to their waiting rental car.

The bar was loud. Obnoxious college students crowded around the televisions that lined the wall. Sports occupied every screen, from basketball to golf highlights from earlier in the day. Most of the place held tables and chairs, none of which stayed in the same positions for more than ten minutes at a stretch. Booths were few, but Morgan locked one down in the back corner. It gave her a full view of the place.

From her perch, Morgan observed the entire dining area. She noted the drunkards challenging each other at the dartboards, and the young lovers making out near the jukebox. A few enjoyed meals at their tables, mostly the seniors of the crowd, who grumbled about better days before the college took over every decent watering hole in the area.

Opposite Morgan's position, she noted a young man sipping at his beer. He wore a low-brim hat. Nervous fingers danced along the edge of the table. A large bag of takeout sat next to him. His gaze was never on the room, or the beer caught in his grip, but the parking lot outside the window. Morgan trailed his attention to a blue pickup truck in the lot. It took up two spots, the back half of the vehicle lost in the shadows.

Afraid of getting dinged up, Morgan thought, even though the truck was nothing but rust spots and bent-in panels.

Morgan's curiosity was interrupted by the arrival of their waitress. She carried a tray of drinks and set them down in the center of the table.

"There ya go," she said with a wide grin. "Getcha anything else?"

"I think we're good for the moment," Ben replied.

The waitress stuck around for a long second until she caught Morgan's icy stare. "Or as good as we're bound to get, at any rate."

"Well," the waitress said, refusing to give Morgan another glance. "You holler if you need a fresh one."

Before the waitress was three steps away, Lizzy reached out and grabbed the Guinness set between them. She took a long slurp of the lager; half the glass vanished in seconds.

Setting it down, Lizzy swiped at her soaked lips. "Not too much of a stereotype, I hope. I'm just thirsty, is all."

Morgan appreciated the woman's candor. Stereotype barely covered the matter. Lizzy's fiery red hair and emerald eyes made her heritage clear.

"Does skulking in the shadows usually have that effect on you?" Morgan asked. The question drew a sharp look from Ben, but he remained silent on the subject. Morgan didn't know whether to thank him or check his pulse. Either way, she knew her luck wouldn't last.

"I was monitoring two suspicious individuals," Lizzy said with a smirk. "For public safety."

"Federal agents, remember?"

Lizzy scoffed. "Oh, I recall. And please don't break out the badge again. It's not your counterfeiter's best work."

Ben started to smile. Morgan raised a finger toward him. "Shut it."

"Fine." He reached for his smoothie. He took a long drag of the fruity concoction, then pushed the glass away. His hands clasped before him. "Emily Wright. Where is she?"

Lizzy shrugged. "Your guess is as good as mine, and about as accurate. She's been missing for eight months. No trace. A ghost in the world."

"And you happen to show up here looking for her," Morgan said.

"You did," the woman shot back. "Someone ran her name through Missing Persons, cross-referencing with Wichita. Wasn't a stretch to make the connection, and head this way for a quick look."

Morgan turned to Ben, who offered her the same knowing stare. "Adler," they said at the same time.

Morgan shook her head. "Real subtle."

Ben chuckled, then shifted back to Lizzy. "How do you stay so well-connected?"

Lizzy lifted her camera from the bench. "Photojournalist. Freelance, but my work has been featured in *Time*, *Newsweek*, the *Post*, and others. The work gives me access to certain things and the freedom to investigate."

She was too young. That was Morgan's first impression when

hearing the woman's credentials. She was way too young to be that far in life. Who the hell was Lizzy really, and what was she doing working the same case as them?

"Freedom to investigate," Ben repeated. "Like missing people? Why?"

"I could ask the same." Lizzy settled the camera on the table. "Why Emily?"

Ben's gaze fell to the table. "It's personal."

"Old flame." Lizzy took a long sip, then set the glass back down. "Got it."

Ben's eyes widened. "No, that's..." He sighed. "She's a friend."

"Right," Lizzy said with a wink. "Since you've come back with nothing from the day, what's your next move?"

Ben fell silent. The confidence he typically carried wasn't present, and his uncertainty won out. Morgan tried to wait, but she'd known their next move since the abandoned townhouse and the emptiness they'd found there.

"We regroup at home," she finally said.

"Morgan?" Ben asked, his gaze thin and angry.

"It makes sense, Ben," she continued. "If the call was her, then we can analyze it further. Figure out what she was trying to tell you."

Ben wanted to yell at her. She could see it in his face, in the way his jaw tightened when she stopped talking. What surprised her was the same animosity came from the young woman on the other side of the booth.

"What?" Morgan asked Lizzy.

"Nothing."

Morgan leaned closer. "Say it, lady. You don't strike me as someone who holds back."

"Good eye." Lizzy inched closer. "You're right. Sounds like the smart play. Also sounds like giving up after one hard day."

"That isn't—"

Lizzy waved her down, clearly not finished. "I'm used to the reaction. Authorities tend to brush off a case rather than put any skin in the game."

"Hey," Morgan snapped. "You don't know anything about us. This isn't some fly-by-night operation."

Lizzy let out a sharp laugh. "Could've fooled me."

Morgan's fist clenched. "You arrogant—"

"Drop it, Morgan," Ben interrupted. His hand settled over hers, bringing it back to the table. "Go ahead then, Lizzy. What should we be doing?"

The young photographer cocked her head to the wall of televisions. Three of the screens shifted from their standard programming for a special news report. The background displayed the campus at Newman College. The photo of a young woman filled the forefront, her name in bold letters at the bottom of the image: MIRIAM PRESCOTT. A single word joined the name.

MISSING

"Well," Lizzy said with an air of superiority that made Morgan cringe. "And this is just me, but you came to find a missing person. So how about we find one?"

CHAPTER TEN

Morgan wanted to scream. The second they left the bar, they should have headed straight for the airport and home. Instead, thanks to Ben's insistence on following the lead of a complete stranger, they made their way back to Lizzy's van, then proceeded over to Newman College.

Ben had made justifications during the drive. A girl had gone missing. A case had landed in their laps, as it had so many times before. Each reason held merit, and each kept her following the rusted-out van in front of her rather than skirting toward the airport for a flight back to Bethesda.

None of them, however, were the truth. Morgan could tell from the glassy stare in her partner's eyes, and the way he practically swooned at the mention of Lizzy. He was still following the lead that had brought them to Wichita. That lead had given them Lizzy, but it also opened the door to new insight into Emily's disappearance.

Morgan didn't need the aggravation, nor the second-guessing when it came to procedure. They circled the outskirts of the sprawling campus until they found the active crime scene. Barricades cordoned it off. A flash of her badge was enough to move the obstruction, and they passed the initial officers without a word other than a nod for the van to be allowed through as well.

They parked close to the scene. Spotlights surrounded a large tent, a temporary command center to coordinate the search for Miriam Prescott. Morgan exited the car. Ben trailed close behind. He reached out to hold her approach to the tent, his head tilted toward the still parking van.

Morgan sighed. Something about Lizzy was off-putting to

her. The young woman was definitely hiding something from them, and she worried about what it meant for their evening. What should have been a straightforward lead was turning into a much larger distraction. Morgan feared the loss of focus would hamper them further.

"This is a mistake, Ben."

Lizzy approached, her camera dangling from her neck. Press credentials swung from a lanyard over the lens. Ben's eyes locked on their new colleague, and refused to peel away for even a second.

"Ben?"

"Huh?" He shook his head, then shrugged. "A mistake? Probably. But we've made worse."

She cocked an eyebrow in frustration. "We don't know a thing about this case. We can't force our way inside--"

"We're offering to help, Morgan. Isn't that what we do?"

Morgan huffed. "Of course, but—"

"Miriam Prescott's twenty. Undeclared, but her schedule is heavy on the psychology side," Lizzy said. "She's the daughter of a City Council member currently seeking reelection. No criminal record. No red flags in her school file. A good kid."

"How did you—"

"Come on, Morgan," Ben said. "She's press. Probably just running a background check."

Lizzy gave a disarming smile to the pair. Morgan saw right through it.

Ben, however, jumped to Lizzy's defense. "Let her do her job."

"As long as she stops trying to do ours," Morgan grumbled.

Lizzy patted Morgan's shoulder. "And spoil your fun? Have at it, Agent."

Morgan stopped. Her first instinct was to twist the woman's fingers back until they snapped. She held back that instinct, as well as her tongue. They made their way through the crowd of cruisers blocking the access road until they reached the narrow sidewalk, just shy of the woodlands where the tent was set up.

"ID?" an officer asked.

Ben pointed to his badge. "FBI. Agents Scrooge and Cratchett."

"Excuse me?" the officer exclaimed in confusion.

Morgan rolled her eyes. She shoved Ben aside. "Dunleavy and Riley."

The officer, a wisp of a man, studied the badge. With each glance, he turned to the sniggering Ben, unsure about whether to give them access. Finally, he shifted away from the entrance to the makeshift command center.

Morgan pushed Ben ahead. "Idiot."

"We could have used any name, and we get saddled with our own," Ben complained. "No creativity anymore."

He turned and flipped the badge in her face. She ripped it from his hand, closed the ID, then jammed it against his chest. "Knock it off."

"Look at what creativity gets you."

"I'll show you exactly what it will get you if you don't put that badge away and pull it together."

The truth was, they had no jurisdiction, they never really did. The DSA always skirted the line with their legitimacy. Most of their actions bordered on the criminal, and with the recent outing of Stallworth and their former operations, they needed to keep their heads down when it came to field work.

Their operational status relied on the falsified documents drawn up during their tenure as official operatives. Zac, unfortunately, had not been the best at making them.

Ben relented. The badge slipped into his pocket. He paused, blocking Morgan's entry further into the tent. Morgan turned back to see Lizzy.

The officer at the door stopped the young woman. "You can't have that camera in here."

"Sure thing." Lizzy lifted the equipment from around her neck and passed it over to him. "Keep her safe. She's not cheap."

The officer held the camera out in surprise. He set it down on the small table next to him, then turned to the growing line seeking entry.

Ben threw an inquisitive look at their new companion. "Really?"

"Happy to help," Lizzy said with a shrug.

The tent was merely a canopy to block the elements. Rain was in the forecast, and if the growing cloud cover was any indicator, the storm would soon be upon them. The right side of the tent remained open to allow access to the woods. Spotlights showcased the line of brush surrounding the route of Miriam's supposed run.

The trio made their way to the open side. Once they were out of sight of the entry guard, Lizzy reached into her pocket and pulled out a small digital camera.

Morgan rolled her eyes. "Yeah. Happy to help yourself."

Lizzy leaned close. "I'm here to help find a missing girl, Agent. Try to remember that."

"Me?" Morgan asked, a hand to her chest. "I might be the only one focused on that."

Ben took the lead. He passed along a pair of gloves to Morgan. They put them on and circled the spotlight. Ben pointed to the branches jutting from the brush.

"Blood." He lifted a single branch. Lizzy's camera clicked to collect evidence. "A number of these are snapped. Like someone fell here."

Morgan nodded. She crouched low. "Boot prints from the road." Her finger noted their positions, three clear impressions. "They stop here, but look..." The steps followed a clear path into the woods.

"More tracks."

Lizzy agreed. "Deeper treads."

"From carrying the body? Ben asked.

"That was our thought," a voice said from behind them. Lizzy tucked her camera up her sleeve and held it in place. Ben and Morgan stood from their searching to greet the newcomer to the conversation.

He stood over six-feet-tall. He was well-built and his uniform hugged his chest. Blond hair shone as bright as the badge clipped to his shirt. He held out his hand and smiled. "Detective Morris Bellamy."

Ben started to reach out. "Scrooge—"

"Dunleavy and Riley," Morgan interjected. She shook the man's hand firmly, then let it drop as quickly as Ben's incessant joke.

"I just called for federal assistance." Bellamy ushered them back into the tent. "You're fast."

"I'm sure we're only the first," Morgan replied.

There were four tables set up along the right half of the tent. A map occupied one of the tables. Communications equipment was staggered throughout the area. Officers worked to coordinate the scene and set up a search pattern. A staging table on the back wall carried a takeout box of coffee and paper cups.

One of the officers noticed Bellamy's arrival and shot over to him. "Detective!" The young man skidded to a halt before them. He held tight to his hat, afraid to lose it. "The roommates are here."

"Thanks," Bellamy said. He turned to Morgan, unable to tear his eyes from her for a second. "Care to join me?"

"Lead the way."

Bellamy headed to the partitions on the other side, with Lizzy at his heels. Morgan waited and caught a grumble from her partner.

"Nice guy," Ben whispered as they joined the rest. "Be nice if he looked at your eyes."

"Jealous much?" Morgan asked with a smile.

"Just professional, Agent Scrooge," Ben said. "Just professional."

The partition allowed some level of privacy. There was a single table and twin chairs. They were both occupied by a pair of co-eds with strawberry blonde hair and knee-high boots. Introductions passed around, informing the group of the girls' names: Harper and Jess.

"She always goes for a run this way," Jess said, terror in her voice.

Harper was more assured, the stronger of the pair. "We told her it's not safe. Her dad mentioned it to her as well. Probably why she did it."

"Any trouble for Miriam?" Bellamy took a soft approach with the girls. There was no reason to suspect them of anything. They had come willingly when called, and their concern appeared genuine. "Did she have any enemies? Boyfriend issues?"

"None." Jess shook her head repeatedly in answer. "Everyone loved Miriam... loves Miriam."

Harper took her friend's hand. "Yeah. Some too much."

Jess' eyes widened. "You mean—"

"Don't you think?"

Bellamy cleared his throat to draw their attention. "Ladies?"

"Sorry," Jess said. "She means--"

"Professor Fletcher," Harper said.

Lizzy took a step deeper into the room. "Daryl Fletcher?"

Everyone turned to the photographer, all curious how she chimed in with that information, and why.

"I... I think so," Jess muttered.

"He always made time for Miriam," Harper said. "He was always there to give her extra help."

"She was struggling," Jess admitted.

Harper scoffed. "Everyone was struggling in his class."

Jess nodded. "But she was his top priority, it seemed."

The girls continued to go back and forth. Information about Miriam slipped out between remembrances of semesters past and other tangential associations. Morgan doubted their connection to the girl's abduction.

Her immediate concern centered on Lizzy, who quietly backed away from the crowd for the main area of the tent. Ben caught Morgan's distraction and turned.

"Lizzy?" he called once they were clear of the interview area. "What is it?"

She didn't bother to answer. Hurried steps carried her to the entry guard. She grabbed her camera, slipped it around her neck, then continued for the road.

Ben moved to follow. Morgan held him back. "Let her go, Ben."

His concern for their newfound companion won out over the case surrounding them. Morgan sighed as Ben pulled away. He trailed Lizzy toward their parked vehicles.

Morgan held back a step, in shock at his behavior. Didn't he see what was happening here? *No*, Morgan thought. Ben didn't have a clue. He was too stuck on Emily to realize Miriam Prescott needed their help.

CHAPTER ELEVEN

Morgan continued to call after him. Ben, however, pressed on after Lizzy. The woman fascinated him. She was so young, yet so completely driven in her mission. Everything she did served others, whether it was in showcasing the truth through her photos, or in rescuing the missing.

He was glad to have her along tonight. For so long, Ben believed himself to be the only one concerned for Emily's safety. He had been the sole searcher in the hunt for his former partner. Now, it turned out there was another, and Lizzy was in it for the long haul... unlike Morgan.

Ben fought back his anger. Morgan tried to be there for him, but her perpetual misgivings—and the need to give them voice—helped no one. It certainly didn't help Emily, and that was the priority. That was why they were in Wichita. The Miriam Prescott business was merely a tangent from the true mission.

Lizzy knew more than she was telling. The way her eyes sparked at the mention of Daryl Fletcher made it clear. Somehow, she was more in tune with the missing. It reminded Ben of his encounter with Cal Cooper—a young attorney with a penchant for seeing ghosts.

Ben pursued Lizzy with the same zeal. She carried some clue, some innate knowledge, about those taken or lost. He needed that information to help in his own search.

"Lizzy?" he called as she reached her van. "What's going on? What's the deal with—"

The back doors flung open. Lizzy climbed inside, but Ben stopped short. Shock and surprise greeted him as the contents of the van were exposed for the first time since their meeting.

"Whoa," he said. "Is this you?"

The entire back half of the van appeared customized. No seats occupied the rear. In fact, the entire structure had been gutted and replaced with something far more useful to the young woman. On one side was a table bolted to the floor. Monitors ran hot along the surface. Radio uplink and more communications equipment sat on shelving above the table. Maps were taped to the back of the front bench seat. Suitcases were tucked beneath, with clothes hanging out of them. A narrow cot was positioned on the other side, a thin blanket folded much too quickly in the corner.

"My humble abode," Lizzy said with pride. "Try not to drool on the paint job."

Ben peered in. With Lizzy in the back, it was too cramped to join her. "You installed all this?"

Lizzy nodded. "Not to mention the killer speaker system for the long road trips." Lizzy snatched some paperwork from the desk, then hopped down to the road. "It keeps me informed."

"For your photojournalism?" Morgan joined the pair, a look of obvious annoyance on her face. The setup in the back of the van didn't seem to help her disposition.

"I'm good at it and love the job, but all this?" Lizzy beamed at her living space. "This is for my true passion: finding the missing."

"That's not your job, lady," Morgan snapped. She pulled Lizzy away from the van.

Lizzy spun around to face the woman, anger in her eyes. "Someone has to do it."

"Authorities can—"

"Barely tackle the paperwork on their desks," Lizzy shot back. "They can't see beyond the face on the poster. They don't see the big picture."

Ben shifted between them. The two women eased off. Morgan huffed. Her doubts crept into every word spoken, and every breath dramatically exhaled. Now she sought to poison any sort of connection with the only help they'd found since arriving.

Ben ignored his partner's reticence. He focused on Lizzy, who gripped the files in her hands tightly. "What is the big picture?"

"Ben, you can't seriously—"

Ben refused to look at Morgan. Their new companion intrigued him. "Tell us. What are we missing?"

"Everything," she said in a quiet voice. "Everyone is when it comes to the missing. Abductions aren't random. People don't simply vanish out of the blue, or run away from lives they've spent decades building. There is a real reason these people disappear. A bigger purpose to why they are taken and not others."

"Like what?" Morgan said with a scoff. Ben tried to calm her down with a raised hand, but she pushed past him. "People are taken, abducted, or just plain run away every day. There's no rhyme or reason to the vast majority of them."

"Spoken like a true authority on nothing," Lizzy replied. "You came into town to find Emily Wright and somehow stumble on another missing person's case? You don't think there's a connection?"

"What connection?" Ben asked. Morgan wanted to chime in. Ben glared at her, silently begging for a moment to hear the fiery young woman out.

Lizzy patted the paperwork in her hand. "Daryl Fletcher."

"He's—"

Ben's hand shot back up, and Morgan settled down. "He's the college professor Miriam's roommates mentioned."

"That's right."

"Bellamy and his team will look into him," Ben continued.

"They won't find anything," Lizzy said. "He'll be dropped as a person of interest almost immediately. He's too smart. He'll have his alibi planned out far in advance. And it will be airtight."

"How do you know?"

Lizzy tossed the files to Ben, who caught them square in the chest. As he opened them up, Lizzy pointed to each report. "Fletcher's been present at several abduction sites over the years. College campuses and the surrounding areas."

"Which he could have been invited to as a guest lecturer," Morgan interjected. She sidled up to Ben and reached for the files.

Ben hesitated for a moment, then passed them along for her to view.

"It's the perfect cover," Lizzy said. "There's no reason to suspect him because he's been invited to the scene."

"That's absurd."

Ben wasn't so sure. He paged through the reports gathered by Lizzy, including a Tucson case from four years earlier. Fletcher took part in a panel discussion on the ethics of humanity. *Must have been a brief conversation.* During his visit, a young man had vanished from his dorm room. Nothing had been missing from the scene, no attempted robbery of any kind, and no sign of a struggle. Police had eventually chalked it up as a runaway, instead of a kidnapping. The boy was never seen again.

That was only one instance. Three more files offered similar accounts. All had taken place around visits from Fletcher. Several questions had been asked of the visiting professor, yet not one person placed him with the victim, and no victim was ever located to implicate the man.

Morgan was right, though. Dozens of other potential suspects existed, people with the means to go through with the crimes in question. Ben passed along the rest of the notes and read his partner's wariness.

"Lizzy?" he asked in a soft voice. "Do you have any hard evidence?"

"That's not how this always works, Ben," she answered with a cocked eyebrow.

"Then why point to him here and now?"

"Because of Emily."

Ben's eyes flared. "What?"

"He was in Buffalo, Ben," she said. "Daryl Fletcher was there the night Emily Wright went missing."

CHAPTER TWELVE

Enough was enough.

Morgan took the entire conversation in stride, letting her opinion known where she could to pull Ben back to the side of reason and logic. She seized Ben by the hand and dragged him away from Lizzy.

They shuffled through the slew of squad cars that filled the narrow inlet on the campus. Ben started to speak, each time interrupted by another sudden jerk of Morgan's hand. She wasn't ready to hear it, not until she offered her own opinion on the night's events.

They were supposed to be partners. More than that, they were meant to be seasoned investigators who helped people in need. Turning to a photojournalist who spouted nothing but paranoia and conspiracy theories was the last thing Morgan thought possible during their visit to Wichita.

Finally stopping a distance away from the lived-in van, Morgan fought for a calm breath. The second she noticed Ben glancing through Lizzy's reports once more, any notion of calm left her.

"Are you insane?" Morgan snatched the documents away from him, then crumpled them between her fingers.

Ben stared at her, aghast. "Me? Morgan, you heard her."

"Heard what, exactly?" Morgan lifted the mutilated paper. "Some ridiculous theory about a conspiracy behind thousands of abductions around the globe? That little chestnut?"

"Fletcher was in Buffalo the same night Emily disappeared," Ben said.

He believed every word of her story without question. To

Ben, Lizzy was the partner he needed, the one who supported him without hesitation and without doubt.

"Ben..."

"He was there!"

"So was the former governor of New York!" Looks shot their way from the officials. Bellamy flipped open the wall of the tent to check on the situation. Morgan seethed. She shot Bellamy a wave, then pulled Ben closer. "Should we be pounding on *his* door about Emily's disappearance too?"

Ben shook his head. She had pushed him too far and knew it the second he ripped away from her. "You're unbelievable. You never thought Emily was here, did you?"

He didn't need an answer to know the truth. She didn't have one, but the doubt had been present the entire time. From the second he'd burst into her room to share the call, everything had fallen so perfectly into their laps after months of agonized silence. Of course, Morgan had doubted the entire lead.

"Ben..." she started, unable to find the words.

"Do you even think she's alive?"

Silence settled between them. Words caught on Morgan's tongue yet fell dead on arrival at her lips. The quiet spoke for her in every way she failed to.

He swatted back the attempt to connect. "For a second, I thought you were with me on this."

"I am," Morgan said as he continued to shift away from her. "Dammit, Ben, I am. But you have to realize the chances of your friend being alive after all this time. They're..."

"She was more than a friend, Morgan," Ben said. His eyes shot daggers through her. They were pained by the loss of not just one partner, but now two. "And she's still alive. She has to be."

He started back to the van. Lizzy didn't have to say another word to pull him to her. Ben's every thought centered on Emily.

Morgan didn't realize the depth of his connection with his former partner. He had always labeled her as a friend, never anything more to intimate the chance for more. Or had she simply been too clueless to read the signs, to see the way even the mention of Emily's name pained Ben because of her absence from his life?

"Ben, come on," she said, giving chase. She circled around

him to cut him off from the van. "This woman is wrong. Doyle is hiding something. She lives in a van connecting dots to some imaginary puzzle. Running from crime scene to crime scene? Does that sound like a healthy person to you?"

"She's trying to help," Ben replied. "She's willing to believe. Which is more than I can say about you."

He pushed through her. Morgan reeled back. "Who?" she called to him. "Who is she helping? Is it Miriam Prescott? Or Emily Wright? Is it any of them, or only herself?"

"Stop." Ben threw his hands in the air. "Just stop it."

Morgan shook her head. "Not until you listen to reason."

"No," Ben said with finality. He held out his hand. Slowly, Morgan let go of the crumpled reports caught in her grip. He took Lizzy's files and tucked them under his arm. "I'm going to look into Fletcher. If he had something to do with Emily, with any of this, I have to know."

Emily came first. She always would in his eyes. Morgan couldn't fight Ben any longer, refused to push him to accept a version of reality that was counter to his own. He needed the chance to find his answers. Ben was always obsessive like that with the work. Tunnel vision, Morgan called it. He referred to it as dedication and never understood the difference.

Morgan's head lowered in surrender. "Do what you have to, Ben."

She left him behind with the van and the curious stares of Lizzy Doyle. There was more to say, but Morgan let it lie between them. The work came first, and they both had their paths to follow.

"Where are you going?" Ben asked.

Morgan's steps carried her farther away from her partner and back to the tent on the side of the road. "There is an actual case here, and one of us should follow it where it leads."

Miriam Prescott was her job now, and Morgan intended to find her.

CHAPTER THIRTEEN

Ben quietly cursed under his breath. Morgan stomped her way to the makeshift command center. She never looked back, never noticed the conflict in his eyes. They were supposed to be partners, equal contributors in decision making. Most of all, she was supposed to have his back. After all their time together, he certainly deserved that much.

That hadn't been the case, however. Instead of following his lead—or even believing in their visit to Wichita—Morgan had done nothing but poke holes in every clue found. She offered none in return.

Ben needed to find Emily, and Morgan couldn't be bothered to get behind the search. Not truly, and not with an open mind and an open heart. She never believed Emily had left the mysterious message on his phone, or that she was somewhere in Wichita. Ben knew differently.

Once Morgan was out of sight, Ben turned for the waiting van. His curses continued. The frustration at their constant arguing brought them nothing but division when they needed to stick together. Rather than push for her help, Ben left her behind.

Lizzy sat along the rear of the van. Her legs kicked out in the air, clearly eager to head out. When he approached, she jumped down. Shutting the doors to the van, she greeted him with a cocksure smile.

"That went well."

"Yeah." Ben rubbed the back of his neck. "She doesn't get it. Emily and I... we were close. I never had the chance to tell her that. I should have been honest with her, shouldn't have let a moment slip by when..." Ben shook his head. He met Lizzy's soulful gaze. "If there is even a chance she's here? I owe it to Emily to see it through."

"I understand," Lizzy replied. She fixed her ball cap, then ran her hand through the hair that escaped down her neck. "I've seen the same look on way too many faces. Including the one in the mirror."

Ben stepped back at her comment. "What do you mean?"

"Not important." Lizzy shook her head and started for the van. "We'll find Emily. You have my word."

Something about Lizzy made it absolutely clear to Ben this was the right move. Her movements and her words carried nothing but confidence. She believed in the mission. She spent every single moment in service to finding the missing people of the world, and here she was doing the same for Emily. Lizzy was on Ben's side, unlike his partner and friend, who could only throw doubt in his path.

Lizzy opened the passenger door for Ben. "We should get moving."

Ben nodded. He stepped up to the seat and settled against the torn cushion. Lizzy shut the door and circled the front.

Opening the window, Ben peered at the tent once more. "I have to do this, Morgan," he whispered. "This is the right move. I hope."

That was what it came down to: hope. Every time he thought about Emily, he believed her to be alive. Where everyone else saw the darker side of the equation, to think there was a chance she had met her end was impossible for Ben. It failed to compute in his analytical mind.

Lizzy jumped into her seat, then turned the key in the ignition. The van struggled to start for a brief second, a prayer clear on Lizzy's lips. The engine roared to life, the entire chassis shaking.

"Fletcher's place isn't far," Lizzy said.

"We do this by the book," Ben said, suddenly wary of their destination. He knew nothing of the man, and the lack of information crashed down on him. If Fletcher had been present the night Emily went missing, Ben needed to know. Part of him, however, still heard Morgan in the back of his mind. "You follow my lead."

Lizzy offered a sarcastic salute. She slammed the shifter into drive. "Let's move."

CHAPTER FOURTEEN

Adler stared at Zac from across the table. The Arcadia Diner was bustling. College groups met to discuss classes and their plans for break. Families enjoyed catching up from the long day before a quiet night at home. Staffers smiled and greeted each of their customers, always aware of who they were and what they enjoyed.

The exception came with Adler and Zac in the corner booth. Water sat before Zac. It arrived with no straw, no ice, and no lemon on the side. All that accompanied the beverage for Zac was a dirty look from the server.

"What was that about?" Adler asked, after a sip from her much-needed coffee.

"I work here," Zac said. "This is my day off."

It didn't answer the question yet had at the same time. Adler had seen the disdain from Zac's subordinates at the DSA. He had been in charge of the entire research division, yet not one person in the entire department had cared enough to call Zac a friend.

Adler understood why to a degree. There was a disconnect between boss and employee. Zac, though, had carried things a little too far at the DSA. It appeared his attitude continued to cause a rift for himself at his current position as well.

"What do you want, Adler?" Small talk was over for him.

Adler failed to answer. She was still too busy staring at him. This wasn't the Zac she had come to know at the DSA. There was no confidence, no arrogance in his posture. Every inch of his body screamed surrender. No fight remained in him.

He looked tired. Part of it must have been the weight loss,

which was clear the moment she had found him. His cheeks were sunken, and his shirt hung loose on all sides. Wrinkles dotted the corner of his eyes. His youthful appearance had faded over the last month, much too quickly to be natural. Something was wrong with him.

"Aren't you going to ask how we found you?" Adler tried to get things back to casual, afraid to push him away too soon. "We—"

"My call to Claire," Zac said matter-of-factly. "She asked me to stop calling. I tried, left her alone for a week while I... sorted things out, but I called her this morning."

Pain filled his eyes. The conversation had obviously not gone well between them. That was no surprise to Adler, who had uncovered Zac's affair with Morgan Dunleavy. That had been another mistake in a long line of them for Zac of late.

Adler reached for him. "Zac..."

He tucked his hand into his lap sharply. "You shouldn't be here, Adler."

"Hey," she said. "You didn't know about Sullivan. What he did—"

"I should have known," Zac said, agitation in his voice. "I watched him, fed him info because I was upset about Metcalf's decisions. I gave him everything, and it cost Lincoln his life. And who knows how many others? No, there are no excuses for me."

"So what?" Adler asked. "You're going to stay here in the boonies for the rest of your life? You don't have to keep running. Come home."

"Home?"

"To the DSA," she continued. "We could use your help."

Zac pushed the water away, then settled deeper into the corner booth. Hope sparked in Adler. Something hid in Zac's gaze, something she'd seen only in the quiet of the DSA's Operations Room.

"Adler, I—"

Adler leaned closer, hoping to give him the necessary push. "We need you, Zac. The Trust is manipulating events on a global scale. If we could find out what they're after, it would go a long way to stopping them."

Zac paused for a moment. Adler's words sank in, but in the silence, his own doubts broke through. "No. I can't help. Sorry."

Adler shook her head. "Listen to me, Zac."

"I'm not that guy anymore." He shifted for the end of the booth.

Adler cut him off. "Yes, you are, dammit."

"You don't need me, Adler."

"Yes, I do," she snapped. She fought back her frustration with a deep breath. "That's why I'm here. I need your help, Zac. Not Metcalf. Not Morgan. Just me."

Zac's brow furrowed. He slumped at the edge of the booth. "Why?"

Adler loomed over him. "I've been tracing a rogue signal ever since Maine. Something in the background, constant yet elusive somehow. I've never seen anything like it before."

Zac's eyes widened. "A signal?"

"Yes," she said. His curiosity was clear. "It cropped up on my scanners when the Cove imploded."

Zac bit his bottom lip, chewing over the information she'd shared. Words slipped out, but were lost in his mutterings and the murmurs of the crowd in the diner. He refused to glance in her direction, refused to give up anything, yet she stuck with him.

"What is it?" she said. "Do you know something about this signal?"

Bloodshot eyes met her. Zac shook his head. "Leave it alone, Adler."

"What?"

Zac left his full glass of water and struggled to stand. "Walk away and stop looking for meaning in every little thing."

Adler scoffed. "How? How can you say that? I'm trying to help you, Zac."

He leaned close. "I'm doing the same. Don't look for me again."

Zac pushed through her and headed for the exit.

"Zac!" she called after him. Adler grabbed some spare change from her wallet. The cash fell to the table beside her still steaming cup of coffee. She was really hoping to finish the much-needed refreshment. Instead, she started after her departing companion.

Kanigher sat at the counter. He sipped at a milkshake. A plate of fries rested in front of him. At the sound of Adler's voice, he turned to see Zac heading in his direction. He stood to block the exit.

"Hey, now," Kanigher said. His hand jutted out, pushing at the charging Zac. "Let's not escalate this, Modine."

"Move aside, you lumbering oaf!" Zac shouted.

All eyes in the diner flew in their direction. All conversations halted. Suddenly, their personal lives mattered little. Everyone held their breath at the confrontation at the front of the restaurant.

Zac's fists clenched tight at his side. Even from behind him, Adler noticed the reddening of the man's cheeks and the back of his neck.

She reached for him. "Zac, we didn't come here to fight."

Kanigher lowered his hand and shifted aside. "Let him go, Adler. He's not worth the effort."

"Exactly," Zac replied. He moved for the door. His eyes caught on the reflective surface. Anger melted away to sorrow. As he pushed the door open, Zac turned back to them. "Forget the signal, Adler. And forget about me."

CHAPTER FIFTEEN

Zac refused to look back. He tucked his head down, shoved his hands into his pockets, then leaned into the blustery wind. Streetlights dotted the area. The former school-turned-bed-and-breakfast loomed at the end of the block, lost to the shadows.

He had barely held it together with Adler. Her arrival had complicated matters. The blame lay with him. His call to Claire had been a stupid move, one he should have known would be traced by those looking for him. The truth was, he assumed no one would bother. Zac wasn't a loose end, or a valuable asset.

The Wellspring Protocol, however, told him differently.

The voice continued to plague him. She whispered behind his swirling thoughts, and had listened to every word Adler shared in the diner. He was getting worse. The program continued to work its way deeper. It was taking over, and the thought scared him.

Little details slipped away. When Adler mentioned the DSA, a moment passed before Zac remembered what the letters stood for. He'd even had trouble recalling what the department meant to him.

Part of him wanted to head back inside. Adler didn't deserve his rudeness. She had come to help him, and he believed her sincerity in that regard. Heading back into the fold, returning to his former life, was what he had wanted ever since the incident at the Cove. Zac would have given anything in the world to join them in Bethesda. To have a chance to help people again at the DSA, while also reconciling with Claire, would have helped put the last month behind him.

The signal, however, forced him to end the conversation immediately. When Adler had brought it up, he felt himself tighten inside—unable to speak to it, and he knew why. The Wellspring had heard Adler as well.

Everything came back to the signal. From his own insane scrawling on the living room of the Vroman home to April's mention earlier that day of the enigmatic threat. She'd made it clear the signal was his only escape from the Wellspring. It was the only way to get any semblance of peace back and reclaim what little life remained for him.

Something buried deep in the protocol fought against telling Zac more about the signal. He needed to find the transference point, some place where he might investigate further, but the information fought against him. The Wellspring caused him nothing but pain whenever he probed too deeply into the programming.

Half the problem was on his end as he fought to keep control of his body. The other half came directly from the Wellspring; its hidden agenda remained locked from view until Zac accepted his new role. He refused to let that happen.

Zac held no doubt the key to his future lay with the signal. He needed to disrupt it and, in effect, silence the information contained within.

At the base of the stairs to the Academy Bed & Breakfast, Zac stopped. His head pounded. April wanted another word, another lecture, to teach him his new role. He had no desire to hear anything from her. No, Zac needed a clear head and the chance to solve this new mystery before him.

Turning away from his room and a night of troubled sleep, Zac headed back to the Ozark Trail. The trail granted a peace that his room failed to offer. He needed that peace to think about the road ahead of him.

It was a road made more complicated thanks to Adler's arrival. If she had found him so easily, there was no telling who else might.

He wasn't safe in Arcadia. Zac wasn't sure he was safe anywhere anymore. But for tonight, Arcadia would have to be enough. He needed the time to think up a plan.

He hoped to hell one would come to him... and soon.

CHAPTER SIXTEEN

Duloc was still out. The sound of his snores trailed Metcalf through the underground complex. His breathing alone sent waves of irritation through her.

Playing the role of Alexa had been a necessity. After letting St. James go the previous week, Nixon had tracked the man's every move for some clue as to his affiliation with the Trust. Duloc had been the man's first call. It had also been his second, third, and forth; Duloc had done his best to ignore the ravings left by St. James at his home and his office. Eventually, Duloc had caved, providing St. James—and, by extension, Metcalf— details of a future party at the hotel, so they could reconnect and get to the bottom of their situation.

From there, Metcalf had one play: to get close enough to the ebullient playboy long enough to infiltrate a Trust stronghold. What he lacked in romantic overtures, Duloc certainly made up for in business acumen.

The basement laboratory was advanced beyond compare. Metcalf recalled Morgan's report of the Cove, and the level of technology that filtered along the walls and in every corner of the complex. The subbasement facility reminded her of the descriptions, with computer terminals notched along every surface. The material used to construct the complex was metal, but unlike any Metcalf had seen before.

"Turn left at the end of the hall." Nixon's voice filled her ear, a constant reminder of his presence on the mission. "Second door on the right."

Metcalf picked up the pace, hampered by the tight red dress. It was another necessity for the mission. She quietly cursed the constricting bodice as she proceeded down the wide corridors. Reaching the door in question, she noted the control console connected to the frame. Her hand wrapped around the knob and shook it.

"It's locked."

"I'm working on it," Nixon grumbled.

Metcalf wasn't surprised to hear the frustration in his voice. For as much as Nixon had intersected with law enforcement agencies in his unending search for the truth about the Trust, this was his first time in the field. Even if said status merely meant a comfy cushion in the back of a van parked across the street, and not in the thick of things, Nixon clearly felt the weight of their task.

"Nixon?" She could hear his fingers working against the keyboard. It was the same sound she'd heard dozens of times from Zac, the man's predecessor. For a second, Metcalf wondered about her former subordinate. Then she pushed aside the brief spell of nostalgia to focus on the task at hand.

"Hang on," Nixon replied. "I need a minute."

The door controls flickered from his tinkering. Still, the lock persisted. Nixon wasn't used to the pressure of an operation. Kanigher had warned her of as much when she'd brought Nixon in. Unfortunately, Nixon was the only man for the job. He had also been the one to bring her the vital intel to make it this far. She owed him the minute.

"Breathe, Nixon." Metcalf backed away from the door. Careful steps, her bare feet cold against the metal tile floor, brought her to the nearest junction. Metcalf scanned the halls for signs of life and found none. Time—and luck—remained on their side for the moment.

"I miss a nice, relaxing hack where no one notices your presence until their bank account is empty or you're three thousand miles away. I'm not built for these high-pressure situations, Susan."

She smiled. "You're sitting in a van surrounded by your favorite toys. Sounds like heaven."

"Using them to navigate through redundant security systems and bypass state-of-the-art locks, so you can access encrypted servers before one or more gunsels spot you and fill you with holes? Yup, no pressure there."

Metcalf cocked an eyebrow. "Gunsels?"

"It's a real word," Nixon shot back. "Look it up."

"Can't," she said. "I'm too busy standing in front of a locked door."

A heavy sigh filled her ear. Typing continued at a feverish pace. The console blinked red twice, then shifted to green. The door beeped and slid loose from the frame.

"There."

"Thank you," Metcalf said.

Nixon's work was spot on. Metcalf stepped through the door into a suite filled with servers. They ran in rows with a clear aisle down the center to navigate through.

"This is nuts," Nixon muttered. "Absolutely nuts."

"I know," Metcalf said. "This level of technology is astounding."

"Not that," Nixon said. "I've seen server rooms. Hell, I've found hidden government bunkers before. Never in person, mind you. What I'm saying is..."

"You were the one who found St. James," Metcalf interjected, reading his train of thought. "You figured out the connection to Duloc, as well as their shared link with the Trust. This was your idea, Nixon."

"Like I said: this is nuts." Nixon continued to tap away. Metcalf, wary of standing so close to the open door, shifted deeper into the server farm. "The others should be here."

"They are otherwise engaged," Metcalf lied. Part of her questioned the solo jaunt as well. Kanigher had been growing restless over the last few days. The man had taken to cooking of late, and the meals had stacked from floor to ceiling in the Bunker's refrigerators. Kanigher needed a mission, something as simple as a grocery run to keep his mind active.

Instead, Metcalf stonewalled him. The same went for the rest of the team. She justified the decision easily. No concrete evidence existed to pursue Duloc. A wrong move may have jeopardized their covert status. There were a dozen more falsehoods hidden behind those pretty sentiments. None of them were the absolute truth. She simply didn't want them with her.

"I have this," Metcalf confirmed, both for Nixon and herself. Holding back intel from the team had caused a rift with the previous incarnation of the DSA, yet she continued to do the same with the current. Opening up, even just a little, was something that remained elusive for her. At least Nixon was with her. She counted that as progress. "Where to now?"

"Third aisle. Left side. The server should open up for you right about—"

Metcalf heard the click and raced to see the server in question. "Excellent work, Mr. Jessup."

"Duloc manufactures high grade servers for hundreds of firms," Nixon said. "It makes sense he would use them for his privileged information."

"And that of the Trust." She looked over the server for an open port. "Where do I hook in for the download?"

"Lighting up the panel now."

The panel blinked three times in bright green. Metcalf took the cue, then removed the USB drive from her handbag. It slipped in without issue. She set to work on the keyboard to input the code as Nixon ran it off through her comm line.

After hitting the Enter key, Metcalf took a step back. "All right. Uploading to you in three, two, one..."

The upload failed, the word painted in bright red letters on the server interface. Metcalf entered the code once more. This time, the server locked down completely. Alarms rang out, and the room dropped to emergency lighting.

"Nixon?"

"Shit!"

"What did you miss?"

"Tertiary security program," he said, his teeth practically grinding at the question. "It prevents unauthorized access via outside source. I should've seen it."

"Too late for recriminations." Metcalf collected their drive, then slammed the server shut. "I need evac now."

Metcalf flew from the room. Rounding corridors, she headed back toward the passenger elevators and the sleeping Duloc.

"Stop," Nixon said. "Movement coming from the elevator."

"Dammit." Steps approached rapidly. The two behemoth guards from their arrival were back. They moved swiftly for her position. Metcalf grabbed the end of her tight dress. She tore a slit along the side to free her legs from the dress' constraint. Then she started deeper into the complex. "Where am I going, Nixon?"

"There's a freight elevator at the end of the hall."

"Which —" She shot around the corner. A quick scan of her surroundings found the elevator in question. "Got it."

"It should get you to the lobby," Nixon said, relief in his voice. The feeling didn't last. "Wait."

"Wait? What is it?"

"Look out!"

Metcalf nearly collided with the pair of guards. They raised their pistols at her approach. Metcalf slammed into the closest one, driving them both back into their respective hall.

With a momentary reprieve, Metcalf raced down the corridor for the elevator. The guards were already recovering from the mild surprise, curses following her frantic steps.

Metcalf dove behind a palate of equipment. Carefully wrapped, it provided a barrier for Metcalf against the guards, who opened fire on her.

"Susan?" Nixon shouted. "Susan, are you —"

"Appreciative of the heads up?" she yelled over the bullets slamming into the palate. "Most definitely. Now open the elevator doors, Nixon."

Metcalf beat her head against the equipment at her back. She didn't bring a weapon. The syringe for Duloc had been risky enough. She couldn't take the chance, not if it meant missing out on finding the complex... and the Trust itself.

The doors to the elevator opened. The shots stopped for a moment, the guards obviously curious about the new arrival to the scene.

"Good work, Nixon," Metcalf whispered. "This is going to be fun. I need you to close the doors now."

"What?"

Metcalf was on her feet. She ran for the open doors. "Now, Nixon!"

Shots rang out, the surprise of the empty elevator no longer a distraction to the two guards. Metcalf used her momentum and dove for the closing doors. She slid against the tile until she crashed into the elevator.

The doors closed. The sound of the bullets pinging against the metal fell to the background as the car started to rise.

"I made it," Metcalf said. "Nixon?"

Static filled the comm line. "Sus... I... can't..."

Metcalf watched as the elevator passed the lobby without stopping. She tapped the button, to no avail. Even hitting the impending floors did little to impede the car's ascension.

"I missed the lobby," Metcalf said. "Are you controlling this, Nixon?"

His voice crackled in her ear. "Use... second..."

The line went dead.

Metcalf cursed, then settled against the back wall of the elevator. She carried no weapon, but that didn't make her any less of a threat.

The elevator reached the penthouse with a quaint ding. The doors opened up to a party. Music filled the air, revelry and laughter flowing from one end of the expansive suite to the other.

All halted at her arrival. Security guards surrounded the car, their guns raised and their voices filled with threats.

"Oh," Metcalf said with her hands in the air. "I think I have the wrong floor."

"Not at all, Susan," a jubilant voice boomed from within the crowd. "You're right on time."

The guards shifted aside; the crowd followed suit as the voice broke through. A lone figure made his way before Metcalf. His hands were clasped tight before him in anticipation. When Metcalf imagined who might be behind the Trust, his name should have climbed to the top immediately. He had always been a snake.

"Well, come on in," David Hollis said with an innocent wave. "I've been looking forward to this for some time now."

CHAPTER SEVENTEEN

Miriam cowered in the corner of her prison. That was the best way to describe the place. It was made up like a bedroom; there was a bed, dresser, and a vanity complete with a full selection of makeup.

They were the accoutrements of a teenage girl's room, and even carried the frilly pink curtains to push the image further, but Miriam didn't see any of it in that innocent light. All she saw was darkness, the menacing shadows tucked in every corner, and especially the one looming in the doorway.

He had stood against the frame for minutes. His breathing was heavy and erratic, as if he might collapse if forced to endure one more moment of silence. Yet he remained quiet throughout, merely watching her from a distance.

The silence made it all worse. For Miriam, there was no clear path of escape. She didn't know what to say, or how to connect with her captor in the hopes of her freedom. She had tried to yell. There had been promises of rescue from her father, from the police, hell even her roommates made the list of potential saviors. The man had refused to rise to the bait.

When words had failed, she'd turned to fighting. She had kicked and clawed at him. That had won her a black eye, a bloody lip, and an hour in what he'd labeled as a time-out.

She'd spent the time weeping in the darkness of the little girl's room. No one knew what had happened to her. No one was coming to save her from her own stupidity.

Everyone had warned her about her jogging route. The campus had held entire lectures on using the buddy system at night, though why they'd spent the money in that manner instead of on proper lighting and security cameras boggled Miriam's mind.

With the man's return, came a new demand. He threw a dress on the bed at her side. It was sky blue with white lace along the trim. "Put it on."

Miriam refused to move. It was more out of abject fear than downright defiance, but held the same effect on her captor.

"Why won't you listen?" The shadow stormed into the room. He lifted the dress and threw it at her. "This is your favorite dress!"

"It..." Her voice cracked and strained. She felt the dress in her hands. "It's not mine."

He screamed. Rage, uncontrolled and swelling from his breast, spilled out of him. He swept his hand across the top of the dresser. Keepsakes and treasures spilled to the floor around Miriam. She tried to defend herself, a hand used as a shield that did little to keep her protected from the sudden onslaught of emotion in the room. Through scared eyes, Miriam noted the music box with the ballerina. Next to it lay a photo, the frame cracked in the corner. A young boy stood beside a younger girl. The girl was wearing the same sky blue dress.

"Why can't you ever just do as you're told?" the man screeched. He bounded for the door. Lifting the large bag of takeout purchased for dinner, the man dumped the steaming contents on the bed. "Why can't we ever have a nice family meal?"

Miriam glanced at the food. Her stomach curdled at the beef patties bleeding on the sheets. She shook her head, then grabbed the photo before her. "I'm not her."

The man moved for her, his fist raised high.

Miriam's eyes snapped shut on reflex. "I don't belong here. Please. You have to see that."

Blood spilled from her swollen lip. His punch sent her crashing against the floor. She wanted to close her eyes forever. Part of her wished her struggle would end right then and there. She never had the strength in her, never saw the potential others noted. Miriam was always afraid, no matter the circumstance.

She fought to sit back up. Swiping at her lip, blood dripped from the tips of her fingers. They dotted the sky blue dress.

Rage-filled eyes softened at the sight. The man ripped the dress from her. Miriam cowered deeper into the corner, prepared for another strike. Instead, the man cradled the ruined dress.

"My fault," he muttered. His head shook in tandem with his hands. "Always my fault."

The man opened the dresser and slipped the dress inside. He patted the fabric; delicate fingers worked to remove as many wrinkles as possible before he closed the drawer once more. He rubbed at his neck in much the same manner—a calming effect that dwindled with each step. Snatching a handful of fries, he popped them between his lips.

"I'm sorry," he said with sad eyes. "I'm sorry I yelled. I'm sorry it has to be this way. That I have to do this."

"You... You don't," Miriam stammered. She inched from the corner.

The man stood, which stopped her movement. Tears ran from his eyes as he removed the belt from his pants. "Yes, I do."

"No."

"Daddy says if you don't listen, you'll learn to, or else," the man said, sniffling back his sorrow. "He says it's why I'm such a good boy. I have to make you listen. So you can be good too."

Miriam reached for the dresser. "I'll put it on. Give me the dress, and I'll put it on. I swear."

He gripped the belt tighter. "I know you will. We're family. We'd do anything for each other. Even if it hurts."

"Please," Miriam whispered. She fell back against the wall, trapped with no chance of escape, no chance of rescue, and no hope of avoiding the pain to come.

The man loomed over her. His presence blocked the light outside until Miriam's entire world fell into shadow.

"I'll love you forever, Sis," he said with a raised fist. "Forgive me."

CHAPTER EIGHTEEN

Daryl Fletcher wandered around his home. He started up-stairs with a shower and a change of clothes. His next stop took him to the kitchen, where he fixed up a snack of some kind. After that, he shifted out of view.

Ben and Lizzy had tried to find a decent vantage point in the backyard of the two-story domicile. After tripping the security light, both at Fletcher's and the neighbor's, the pair resigned to moving across the street. They stuck close to the van; the pretense of car trouble gave them time for their stakeout.

Ben tried to stay focused on the house. The brief glimpses of Fletcher failed to impress him. He appeared to be nothing more than the consummate professor—a man with a job and a life all his own. There was nothing deeper to it.

The stakeout made Ben restless. He wanted to act, to barrel through his growing doubts about the man. The rain didn't help his spirits. The storm had grown from a few scattered showers to a thunderstorm. Cracks of lightning snapped across the skyline, and his umbrella failed to protect him from a rain that had shifted almost sideways in its approach.

The storm played its role, but Lizzy pushed Ben's buttons further. It was in each stolen glance, between the many photos taken. What she caught in her lens looked to be nothing more than closed curtains and the exterior of the property. The obstacles failed to deter her, or her own ambitions for their trip to the Fletcher home.

"This is downright exciting," Lizzy intoned. She lowered her camera and pointed across the street. "We could—"

"We wait," Ben replied. He pretended to glance at the van's

engine. Even if the damn thing truly died on him, Ben wouldn't have had the first clue how to fix it. When he turned to Lizzy, she was smiling at him.

"Come on, Ben."

"Listen," he said with the shake of his head. "You might believe he's guilty, that Fletcher is responsible for abducting the Prescott girl, but we need more than belief to nail him to the wall."

"I know," Lizzy said. "But asking pointed questions will get us nowhere."

"As you've mentioned."

"This isn't just about the Prescott girl, Ben," Lizzy said. Her hand rested on his. "Don't forget about Emily. Not that you ever could. Sorry. I don't know why I said that."

A nod escaped him. "No. You're right. I can't forget her."

Morgan had been right in that regard as well. It hadn't been Miriam's abduction that had brought Ben to Fletcher's home in the middle of a storm. It had been the mere mention of a connection with Emily. Was his focus that far off? Had he lost all objectivity with this case, and buried every tangible lead in the hope that Emily might be found?

Ben closed the hood of the van. He tilted his head to the bus shelter on the adjacent sidewalk. Lizzy followed, using her body to protect her equipment. They tucked deep into the waiting terminal and shook the rain from their freezing forms.

"Who was it for you?" Ben asked.

Lizzy's eyes widened. Her gaze fell to the pool of water accumulating in the gutter. "It's not—"

Ben shifted closer. "Come on, Lizzy. It takes one to know one. You basically said as much. So who did you lose?"

Lizzy lifted her camera once more. She attempted to turn away from Ben for more photos of the Fletcher home. His hand jutted out to block the lens. Lizzy sighed, then settled against the back of the shelter.

"My brother," she said. Her eyes never met his. They stared off into the storm, lost to memory. "Patrick was two years older than me. We were inseparable, especially after we lost our parents. I was away at school. A waste of time, I always said, but we talked every day."

"Any money troubles? Depression?"

His questions snapped her back. Irritation filled the green of her eyes. "He had a good job and a stable relationship. They'd talked about marriage, but he was too young for that. He had a good life, Ben."

"So what happened?"

"We had a fight," Lizzy said. "I wasn't around as much, yet we seemed to fight more and more. It was always just little things. Cleaning—not my strong suit. My career was another sticking point. He hated my photography even when it was just the hobby of a teenager. I stopped calling for a bit after our last argument. By the time I did reach out, it was too late."

"He was gone."

"Taken," Lizzy corrected.

"Were there signs of a struggle?" Ben asked. "Some kind of—any kind of—evidence?"

"None," she whispered. "Nothing at all."

"Then how do you know he didn't just—"

"He wouldn't do that," Lizzy snapped. Her face flew inches from his own. Dripping rain joined her spit as she spoke. "Not to me. He wouldn't. He was taken, Ben. Like Emily, and Miriam, and so many others. I know it, and I'm going to find him. I have to find him."

Lizzy's chest heaved. She dropped to the bench in the shelter. There were more questions to ask, more to hear of her tale, but Ben let it all rest between them. The storm took over and, with it, the silence.

Ben shifted to the curb, away from the reeling young woman. He finally saw it, what Morgan had figured out about Lizzy almost immediately. He saw the hurt little girl who had spent years trying to explain away a tragedy. Her brother was gone, and she'd failed to accept the circumstances behind the event on every level.

No grand conspiracy existed. There was only a kid who needed to find her brother. Lizzy needed to make up for the arguments of the past, and understand why she was the one left behind. None of it made sense to her, so she'd concocted her own theory—a grand mystery to be solved.

Ben was an idiot to listen to Lizzy, a greater idiot for ignoring Morgan's concerns. "Lizzy, I think we should go b—"

His words were cut short by a scream. It rang out from the

Fletcher home, but did not belong to the man who owned the property.

It was a woman's scream.

CHAPTER NINETEEN

"Stay here."

"Ben—"

"Do it!" Ben was on the move before the scream ended. He raced across the street. His sneakers splashed in the puddles, coating his pants. The rain didn't weigh him down. Pushing through the wind brought on by the storm, Ben headed for the Fletcher home.

By the time he reached the stoop, his gun was in hand. He bolted up the steps, a slight pause at the door. It was only for a second as another scream erupted from inside. Ben kicked out at the handle-side of the door. The lock splintered from the blow. Before the door slammed back against the wall, Ben was through and ran deeper into the darkened domicile.

Speed was Ben's primary concern, to reach the source of the scream as quickly as possible. So when he collided with a table on the side of the narrow corridor, Ben fell to the ground. The breath jolted from him on impact. He clutched tight to his weapon to keep it in hand.

Quietly cursing, Ben scrambled to his feet. He rushed down the rest of the hall. Light flickered from the back room of the home. Ben's pace slowed when he reached the corner, when the third scream filled the air.

Ben leaped from the safety of the corner, his weapon raised to chest level. "Hands in the air, Fletcher! Federal agent! You're—"

Lizzy shot around the corner. Light flashed from her camera as she snapped picture after picture. "Got you, you son of a—"

Ben held out his hand to stop her.

"What?"

Fletcher sat on the couch, terror on his face. Ben wished it was because of the movie playing on the massive screen along the far wall, or the ominous music booming from the soundbar on the man's entertainment system. Fletcher's fear came from the gun pointed at him, and the presence of uninvited strangers in his home.

"What the hell?" Fletcher screamed. Popcorn ran down his shirt, the bowl upended by Ben's arrival. Fletcher knocked away the kernels as he stood. Reaching for the remote, he paused the film on the screen. The young actress was frozen in mid-scream, the masked killer with the carving knife almost upon her. "Who the hell do you think you are?"

Ben lowered his gun. "Federal agent, sir. I..."

"That doesn't give you the right to..." Fletcher fought for the words, his night ruined by Ben's intrusion. Ben didn't bother to hear the rest of the man's angry ravings. He was too busy condemning himself for not using his damn brain. He wondered if he even knew how to use it anymore.

Morgan had warned him. She had told him what would happen with Lizzy almost to the letter. Yet he'd failed to consider the possibility. Ben tucked his weapon away.

"What are you people doing in my home?"

Ben sighed, his hands on his hips. "I get asked that question more often than you'd think."

"Ben," Lizzy interjected. "You can't seriously be thinking—"

"Do I know you, young lady?" Fletcher moved for the entrance to the living room. He flicked on the lights. Ben and Lizzy squinted to adjust to the sudden illumination, hands covering their faces for a moment. When Lizzy's hand fell away to her camera, Fletcher pointed at her. "I remember you."

"Oakland," she confirmed.

"That's right!" he exclaimed. The anger returned to his voice.

"Oakland?" Ben's eyes bore down on his companion, who refused to look his way. "You've met him before?"

"Two years ago," Lizzy said.

"You never said anything about that."

Fletcher scoffed. "I can guess why. She accused me of kidnapping someone!"

"You—" Ben stopped. Lizzy had her own past with Fletcher. It was why she knew how his interrogations had gone previously. She had been one of the people doing the questioning.

"He was involved then, and he is now," Lizzy said. "Admit it."

"You're a lunatic," Fletcher snapped. "I want you out of my house now! Both of you!"

"Now, sir—"

Fletcher snatched up the phone from the counter. "I can have the cops here in five minutes."

Ben shook his head. "That won't be necessary."

"No," Lizzy shot back. "Let him call. They'll have plenty of questions for Fletcher about Miriam Prescott."

"Miriam?" Fletcher asked. "What happened to Miriam? Is she—"

"Don't play with us!" Lizzy shouted. "We both know you took her."

"She's missing?"

Ben read the man's eyes. They never wavered, never blinked. Sadness filled them as well as the rest of his face. His shoulders slumped at the news, his cheeks sank, and his hands shook. This was not the man behind an abduction, but one who had just received the worst news possible.

"We're sorry to interrupt your film, sir," Ben said. His outstretched hand helped Fletcher lower the phone back to the counter. "We'll be going now."

"Ben?" Lizzy pleaded. She grabbed at his sleeve, her eyes locked on Fletcher. "You can't. You can't just walk away. He—"

Ben pointed to the open front door. "We're leaving. Now."

CHAPTER TWENTY

Morgan fought to concentrate on the room. Over a dozen people sat in on the briefing. There were deputies from the county, officers from the local precinct, and campus officials willing to lend a hand with their own knowledge of the grounds. A phone was set on speaker, and the voice of Miriam Prescott's father boomed between sobs. The man, a City Council member of some repute according to the local boys, worked his way through his grief rapidly. Threats mixed with pleas, all of which the group did their best to ignore to focus on the task at hand.

What the small gathering didn't include were the boots already involved in the search. Teams scattered the area, trailing the disappearance of the young woman. A clock sat in the corner of the makeshift command center. It was set as a stopwatch depicting the time elapsed since Miriam's abduction. The fourth hour had just passed. Each minute brought with it more chance for failure.

Bellamy worked to keep people motivated. His boisterous voice matched his physique, his steps lively through the command center. Frequent glances toward Morgan notwithstanding, she was impressed by his investigatory tactics, and his ability to stick with facts. His confidence and hope helped lift the room.

"We have sweeps running northeast in a long arc," he said from the front of the room. Sprawling maps were posted along a board behind him. Red dots marked the positions of the search teams, which he pointed at in turn. "There's a ridge about four miles out that should act as a natural barrier to keep our kidnapper pinned in. If he's in that area, we've got him."

Morgan tried to shake her distractions away, but they clung

on tight. For as much as she heard from Bellamy, he was not the one she wanted to speak with at the moment. Ben was out there on his own. His idiocy had led him astray yet again, a constant theme of their time together since his return to the fold.

Emily was a blind spot for him. Morgan had no idea the depth of Ben's feelings for his former partner. She should have asked about Emily long ago. Now, learning of his emotional stake in the case, Morgan realized anyone else was better suited to handle the case.

Still, she had come with him to Wichita. She had promised to support him in his hunt for his friend. She could sense Ben's anxiety over the affair. He worried no one would be left to look for Emily if anything happened to him. Morgan wouldn't let that happen, but his obsession took things too far, as usual.

Morgan had tried to tell him as much, attempted to get him to see the truth of the matter, but had failed. Her communication skills always pushed people away rather than brought them together.

Morgan finished her cup of coffee, savoring the sugar-filled base with eyes closed. It helped to snap her awake and also shed some of the chill from the pounding rain outside. The tent wavered with each crash of the wind, but it held against the elements.

With the arrival of the storm, time became even more a factor in the hunt. Going off tracks in the woods was fine when the weather agreed. Once the rain started, all hope of a quick solution diminished.

A shadow grew over Morgan. She glanced up to see Bellamy at her side. "Agent Dunleavy? You still with me?"

She wondered how long he had been standing there, and how much information had been lost in her daze. "I'm sorry?"

Bellamy smiled and helped her to her feet. "You seemed out of it. Thought I'd check in, and see—"

"I'm fine," she replied. She tried to give herself some space. Chairs boxed her in on all sides. "I'm with you. Yes. I am."

"Good," he said with a slight laugh. "I could use your opinion on—"

"Detective!" a voice shouted from the other side of the tent. Bellamy shifted to face the young officer. Morgan took the opportunity to push in her chair to gain some breathing room.

"What is it?"

The officer pointed to the road where two more cruisers joined the festivities. "We have some fresh faces ready to help."

Bellamy nodded. The new attendees wore rain slickers and wide-brim hats. He threw a welcoming wave in their direction. "I'll be right with them."

The officer took off. Bellamy took a step to follow, then shifted back to Morgan. "Join me?"

She hesitated, unsure what she could offer the conversation. For as much as she wanted to help, Morgan remained the least qualified person in the room. Her inexperience with the terrain, and the distraction of her wayward partner, hampered her abilities.

"Sure, I—"

"Detective!"

Bellamy rolled his eyes. "What?"

The middle-aged woman in uniform stepped forward. She was followed by two others, and all carried a stack of reports. "These just came in from the precinct."

"Pass them along," Bellamy said. There were plenty of hands on deck in the tent. "Then I want you to join the newcomers in the search. Agent Dunleavy?"

Morgan took the files in hand. "I'll take these. You go ahead, Bellamy."

"You sure?" He was clearly hoping for a different response.

"Positive."

He paused for a moment, then tipped his hat toward her. "Thanks."

"All right, gather around," Bellamy called to the growing group. He stepped out into the storm and the others huddled beside him. "I'll try to keep this short."

Morgan turned away from the welcome speech. The stack of paperwork settled on the table. It appeared to be traffic cam feeds from around the area. Bellamy's focus was on the wooded areas surrounding the campus, but he appeared intelligent enough to welcome a variety of theories.

"Want me to run through these?" one officer asked.

Morgan threw the young man a disarming smile before shaking her head. "I'll take care of them."

"Think there's anything useful in there?"

Morgan sat and lifted the first from the pile. "There's always a chance."

"Right." The officer stalked off for the coffeepot. Hope was in short supply. Morgan didn't have the charm of Bellamy to lift the spirits of those around her. All she had were the reports from the last few hours.

Morgan thumbed through each one. Traffic cam feeds were collated by location. The one with the most promise appeared at the main entrance to the campus. Using one of the open laptops, Morgan inputted each license plate she ran across. The first four came back with no direct hits.

The fifth needed no explanation. It was a cargo van. The scarlet-haired driver gripped tight to the wheel as she passed by the campus for the residential area where they had initially met.

"Doyle," Morgan said through clenched teeth. It still stung her that Ben's trust fell with Doyle in seconds what had taken months to build between the two of them. "Guess that makes sense."

Refusing to bog herself down with the distraction, Morgan moved on. She shoved Lizzy's image into her pocket. For ten minutes, no viable leads cropped up from the images. It wasn't until she came across a dark blue truck that she stopped herself.

"Why does this look familiar?" she asked quietly. The man behind the wheel was haggard, but through the growing facial hair, she noted his youth. His eyes were frantic and wide. "Him too. Where have I seen—"

The takeout bag.

At the restaurant, Morgan had seen the man in the corner. He'd been focused on his truck outside, like he couldn't let it out of his sight for even a second. On the table there had been a takeout bag large enough for more than one person.

Morgan clutched tight to the image as the truth crystallized for her. "It was you, wasn't it? You took her."

CHAPTER TWENTY-ONE

Morgan raced to the printer. Everything attached to the license plate from the photo in her hands transferred to the device, the system slow to process her command. She tapped feverishly along the edge of the printer. With each passing second, her movements became more and more hostile until she slapped the damn device into action.

Paper whirred. The connection was tough because of the location, made worse by the growing storm. They were all excuses in Morgan's mind. More excuses were the last thing she wanted to hear. The profile shot out by the printer sat in front of Morgan for a long moment.

All doubt fled from her: this was the perpetrator. All her misgivings about being in the tent and working the case faded the second she saw his face and read his name in the report. Morgan snatched it from the tray.

"Bellamy!" She hurried from the tent into the driving storm. Officers milled about. Most waited for a word from the search parties. Others coordinated with local precincts in case any news came over the wire. Bellamy stood just shy of the initial lead—the blood on the shattered brush long since washed away by the rain.

Morgan skirted between other law enforcement officials to get to Bellamy's side. She pulled at his shoulder for his attention. "Bellamy, I—"

"Detective!" another voice bellowed from across the road. Bellamy glanced at Morgan, then continued to the sound of the officer's voice. The young man stood halfway within the tent, a phone close to his ear. "There's a call coming through. It's the search party!"

"Which one?" Bellamy asked. He was already moving for the tent.

"Wait, Bellamy, I..."

The man shook his head, a finger raised to give him a moment. Morgan settled, frustration rushing through her body. It certainly helped fight back the cold of the rain, but did little to comfort her.

"Which one?" Bellamy repeated.

"Doug's," the officer said. "Um, I mean, Officer Hardin."

It was the first team to make their way into the woods. Morgan recalled the information from Bellamy's briefing, and from the map on full display in the tent. Three men accompanied Hardin, all armed and ready for a fight if need be.

"I'll be with you in a second, Agent Dunleavy," Bellamy said without looking. His hand reached for the phone, and the officer passed it over. "This is Bellamy."

He shifted deeper into the tent. As he listened, more personnel entered. They surrounded the call; each waited impatiently for word from Bellamy.

"You're sure?" he asked into the receiver. He pushed through the crowd for the nearest table. Grabbing at a pen, Bellamy started for the map. "Give me your coordinates."

He waited for the response, a mix of hope and anxiety clear in his big, brown eyes. With each word spoken from the other end, Bellamy nodded. Everyone held their breath for news.

"Sit tight," Bellamy said. He circled an area on the map, then spun to greet the entire room. "We're coming to you."

He hung up and tossed the phone to the officer who had answered the call. Bellamy cleared his throat, a hand in the air. "Okay, people. Settle down and listen up."

The tent filled quickly. Murmurs rose and fell the moment they caught sight of Bellamy. Morgan filtered through the group, forgotten in the mix.

"Our team at the ridge found fresh tracks," Bellamy announced. "One with deep impressions and a steady clip. They most likely belong to our perp. The other set of tracks were staggered, and even dragged in other places."

Smiles broke out in the group. Two sets of tracks meant Miriam was alive. There was still the chance of rescue.

Bellamy caught their attention once more. "Now I need all hands on deck. We're going to sweep ahead of the trail and link back up with Hardin's team. If we do this right, we should be able to surround this monster before he knows we're there."

Nods of approval flowed through the crowd. Morgan, however, remained cautious at the plan. Silence slowly filled the tent. No one questioned the new intel.

"Let's move it, people!"

Groups formed. Circles tightened as each prepared to enter the forest to find the missing girl. Only Morgan remained stationary. She waited for the crowd to disperse. Bellamy peered toward the map once more, then headed for the exit.

"Bellamy, wait," Morgan called after him.

"I can't, Agent," Bellamy said. He tipped his hat to her. "There's a girl out there and —"

"I know," she said. She tucked the traffic report, and everything she had uncovered, into her pocket. "What if this is the wrong lead to follow?"

Bellamy's eyes widened. The mild-mannered professional vanished, and he appeared disgruntled at even the possibility of being wrong.

"You're kidding, right?"

"No, I —"

"This is the only lead I've got," Bellamy said. "And with the evidence at hand, I think it's the right call."

Morgan understood. There was a clear sign of people in the woods, tracks to trail back to their position. Who was Morgan to argue with such evidence?

A slow nod escaped her. "Yeah. Okay."

Bellamy hitched his thumb toward the waiting forest. "You coming?"

"I have to follow up on something," Morgan replied. "Good luck out there."

Disappointment filled his face. "You too."

Bellamy joined up with the crew outside. He belted out orders to the different teams. His natural leadership skills were to be commended. His listening skills, though, clearly needed some work.

Of course, Bellamy wasn't the only one with that issue. Everyone rushed around, the lone lead their one strand of hope in finding the girl alive.

Morgan stood, ignored and alone in the tent. No one looked in her direction. No one questioned the report she retrieved from her pocket.

The young man in the picture stared back at her. His name was Kevin Drake. Twenty-three-years old, Kevin lived just outside the city limits. She checked with campus records. Kevin wasn't a student and never had been. So why was he caught on the campus traffic cam earlier that evening?

It was worth a look, but not worth arguing about with Bellamy or the rest. Instead, Morgan grabbed her phone to call Ben. She was about to tap on his number when she thought better of it. Ben was too lost in his own case.

Morgan switched to her messaging app. She shot off a quick text, then slipped the phone back in her pocket. Tucking tight to her jacket, Morgan headed into the rain for her car. Frantic steps carried her deeper into the storm; thoughts of a desperate and scared Miriam Prescott drove her forward.

CHAPTER TWENTY-TWO

Ben was livid. He stomped back across the street from the Fletcher home. Lizzy's van remained parked against the curb on the far end of the block. When he passed it, he kicked at the tire. It was all he could do to keep from screaming.

It had taken time to calm Fletcher down. They had shattered the lock on his door and destroyed any chance at the man having a peaceful evening. Despite everything, Fletcher had accepted their apologies. There had been surprise in his voice over the news about Miriam, and a promise had been made to pray for her safe return.

The man's attitude was a godsend for Ben; the last thing he needed was for the authorities to get involved. His badge might have afforded him some understanding, but upon scrutiny, that would have instantly evaporated.

Ben certainly deserved a berating from Morgan. Everything she had warned him about had come true. Lizzy was no savior. She wasn't going to magically make Emily appear, yet somehow he'd believed the young woman capable of anything and everything.

Her conviction had made him a believer, as if words were evidence. Her theory alone should have set Ben off. Instead, he'd held out hope she was right—that the missing were somehow connected in a larger puzzle, and Emily was stuck in the middle like a cog in a hidden machine.

Months of searching had offered no answers. Just thinking about how long Emily had been missing made Ben's blood boil. He clenched his fists tight in front of him, then collapsed along the bus shelter near the van. Eight months and there was still no end in sight.

Ben pushed past his swirling thoughts and glanced up to find Lizzy looming over him.

"Ben, listen—"

"No," Ben snapped. He jumped to his feet and shook his head. "I think I'm done listening to you, Lizzy. It took everything I had to calm Fletcher down enough to stop him from calling the cops on us."

"I bet it did," Lizzy said with a huff. She threw a thin glare back at the house across the street. Fletcher stood at a window on the second floor.

"Stop it," Ben said. He grabbed her arm and walked her away from the Fletcher home. "You're not even hearing me, are you? I told him what happened and you know what he said? He would pray for Miriam's safe return."

"Ben—"

He held up a hand, refusing to let her in. "All that man ever wanted was for her to succeed at school. To break out of her shell because she was so shy."

"He's lying!" Lizzy shouted. "He's said the same thing to the authorities dozens of times. This is who he is. He's involved. He has to be."

"Why? Why does he have to be involved, Lizzy?" Ben asked. He wanted to shake her, to wake her up from her delusion. "So he fits your little puzzle? So everything makes sense to you and only you? It's time to wake up. You were wrong. We were wrong."

Ben started to walk away. That was the crux of his argument: his own culpability in their actions. He never should have left Morgan. He never should have become so embroiled in Lizzy's fantasies that he couldn't see them for what they were. They were the dreams of a kid, trying to make sense of her brother's disappearance. None of it was real.

"Ben, you don't..." Lizzy moved to follow. "What about Buffalo? What about Emily?"

"That's enough!" Ben yelled. He spun on his heels. His hands flew up, an invisible wall to keep her back. "There is no big picture and no grand conspiracy. People disappear. People are taken from us and we might never know why, but it happens and we have to move on. We have to live our lives no matter how empty they seem for a time."

His words struck her down. She reeled back a step. Swiping at her eye, Lizzy shook her head. "No. I can't. Patrick—"

"Is gone," Ben said. "But Miriam Prescott might not be. That's what should have been our priority. Morgan tried to tell me, but I was too stuck on my own selfish cause to listen."

Ben sighed. Morgan was right about everything of late. It wasn't out of some desire to see him fail. She had been poking holes since their arrival in Wichita, but it hadn't been to dismiss his search. She had been trying to prepare him for the bad news at the end of the journey.

They were the doubts of a friend trying to soften a forthcoming blow. They were the words of a partner.

Ben reached for his phone. He needed to check in with her, to make amends for his terrible behavior of late. A missed text waited for him when he unlocked his phone.

The message was short and sweet, just the way Morgan liked it. There was an address listed and a single name: KEVIN DRAKE.

"Morgan," Ben muttered.

Lizzy shifted to his side, concern in her eyes. "What is it?"

Ben held the phone out for her to see. "She found a lead."

"We have one right here," Lizzy said. "All we have to do—"

Ben didn't bother to listen to more. The argument was a waste of time, especially if Morgan needed his help. He started down the block. Rain poured down. The storm surged, coating his entire body in seconds. Still, Ben fought to input the address into his phone for directions while at a full run.

"Ben, wait!" Lizzy called after him.

"She needs me!" he bellowed without looking back. He refused to slow for even a second. "I won't let her down again."

CHAPTER TWENTY-THREE

Ben raced down the street. There was a break on the Prescott case, a case Lizzy forced on the pair of strange agents to prove their credentials. She had used the case to see if Ben and Morgan were worthwhile investigators. More than that, she'd wanted to know what kind of people they were—if they cared as much for the missing as she did.

They continued to work the case. Lizzy, meanwhile, stood still. The world kept spinning, yet she remained rooted to her spot across from Fletcher's home.

He wasn't involved in the Prescott case. Any connection to Emily Wright's disappearance seemed strained and circumstantial. It sure as hell wasn't currently relevant, not when compared to the abduction of a twenty-year-old co-ed.

Lizzy ripped off her hat and squeezed the brim. A scream escaped her, and she tossed the ball cap to the ground in frustration. It skidded down the sidewalk until it settled against the van's tire. She stared at the cap, the faded emblem looking right back at her. There were twin dusty stains on both sides of the brim. She remembered the fall that left the marks, as well as the small tear along the top. They were memories of her brother, the reason the hat was so important.

The reason everything she did was so important.

Lizzy collected the hat. She held it close, then threw the cap inside the back of the van before climbing in after it. Her notes were on full display along the left-hand wall. They all centered on Fletcher. She had been so sure of his guilt.

Glancing at the man's house, she caught his silhouette against the second-story window. His eyes were lost to shadow, but she knew he watched her closely. Was he truly saddened over the news of Miriam Prescott's disappearance? Or was it fear in his eyes at almost getting caught for his involvement in the crime?

She couldn't be wrong. Fletcher must have committed the crime, committed some crime that connected with Miriam's abduction. There had been too many coincidences in his past, too many close proximities to the same situation, all spread out over the country. Fletcher was involved.

Yet, what if she *was* wrong? Ben followed a lead to the true criminal, or so he believed. Lizzy wasn't sure what to believe anymore. If she was wrong about Fletcher, what else had she missed over the years?

It always came back to Patrick in the end. Her brother had been the center of her life. They'd fed off each other's successes and raised each other up from their miseries. When he'd disappeared, a hole had been ripped in Lizzy's heart. She filled the void with work, with the almost crusade-like mission of finding those taken.

There had to be a reason for their abductions. Someone was behind them, something bigger that people couldn't see — or didn't want to see. The world refused to look deeper into the problem, the way she had over the last four years.

"People wouldn't just leave," she muttered under her breath. Still, Ben's criticism echoed in her mind. It wasn't truly people that lay at the heart of her concern. It was Patrick. Being wrong about Emily meant there was every chance that she was wrong about Patrick: that Patrick hadn't been taken, but simply left her. "He wouldn't have done that."

Lizzy looked over every note still hanging on the side of the van. "He wouldn't have done that!"

Her hands shot out and pried the notes loose. Fingers squeezed the images. They tore at the reports and the research pulled together. Paper flew away from her into the storm. The wind picked up some and carried them along the street. Lizzy watched her work spin through the air and disappear into the growing storm.

Frustration fell from her. Lizzy drew in long, deep breaths. This wasn't the time to fall apart. Ben was wrong about Patrick and Emily. He was wrong about what she knew to be true at the heart of the missing. Ben had been spot on about one thing, however.

Patrick was gone. Emily as well. Their cases were older and could wait. Miriam could not. If there was a way to save her, Lizzy had to try.

Lizzy jumped out of the van, her feet splashing along the pavement. She took one last glance at the Fletcher home. The shadow remained in the window. He would have to wait, as well.

The back doors slammed shut. Lizzy moved for the driver's seat, her keys dangling between her fingers. She secured her ball cap and hopped into the van. The engine rumbled to life, a roar against the storm.

Lizzy started after Ben's path. He hadn't made it far, and she caught up with him in a matter of minutes. His sneakers were soaked, his hair matted down by the pouring rain. Lizzy sidled the van up next to him. She rolled down the passenger-side window.

Ben paused, a curious look on his face as he fought to catch his breath.

Lizzy shot him a smile and cocked her head to the less-than cozy seat. "Need a lift?"

CHAPTER TWENTY-FOUR

Morgan parked down the street from the Drake residence. Streetlights dotted the area in sparse intervals. Morgan kept the rental car in the shadows almost a mile away. She'd turned off her headlights a mile before that. The moment she exited the car, her heart started pounding in her chest. She tried to curtail her trepidation with slow steps toward the home.

The property was large—a suburban family's dream. Open fields spread along the sides and front of the lot. Trees ran along the left-hand side: a natural barrier from the neighbor's home. A row of bushes marked the other side, a driveway trailed the brush toward the house in the center of the wide expanse.

Cracked siding and dusty windows marred the home. What had no doubt been a beautiful place to live was in a state of disrepair. Panes of glass were broken. The storm door refused to latch and beat against the frame.

Morgan idled at the edge of the property for a moment. The home was two stories with plenty of rooms to explore: plenty of places to hide a young girl. She needed a plan, but fate intervened.

A car turned along the road. They headed back the way Morgan had come from. Their headlights were bright and showered the lawn. Morgan barreled for the darkness, afraid to be caught by any possible onlookers from the residence.

Morgan stuck close to the tree line to keep out of sight from both the car and the home. When she reached the edge of the domicile, she tucked under the first-floor windows. Sound, muffled and garbled, slipped through the shoddy windows from a television set.

Morgan crooked her head around the frame for a peek inside. Light beamed from the living room, a shadow sprawled along the wall. A young man sat on the couch across from the screen. His weight caused the cushion to deflate beneath him. His hands dipped into the takeout bag from the diner, pulling out random fries without taking his eyes off the screen. Morgan recognized Kevin Drake immediately, then moved away from the window.

Convinced at the man's distraction, Morgan continued to scan the perimeter. She circled around the back of the home and stopped. A two-story garage took up most of the property. The windows on the upper floor were boarded shut, providing no clue about what hid within.

The space between the home and the garage was taken up by what had once been a basketball court. Its net, long-since rusted, hung limply to one side. One swift gale at the appropriate angle would finish it.

The home was occupied and the most likely target. The garage, though, held its own prospects. Morgan shifted her focus, her gun firmly in her grasp. Two steps in, she realized her mistake.

A spotlight off the back of the house caught her movement. It switched on and illuminated the yard. Morgan rushed for the shadows along the side of the domicile.

The back door opened. Morgan inched to the corner. Kevin was haggard, his beard overgrown and unkempt. It made him look much older than his twenty-three years, his gut not helping matters. He glanced around the yard, then took a sip of his drink.

"Sensor," he muttered. "I can fix it, Dad. Like you said, a boy should be able to fix things. I can fix it."

The door closed. The lock slipped back into place loudly. Morgan let out a long breath, and relief flooded her. She held her position for over two minutes before the spotlight switched off.

Darkness returned to the yard. Morgan left the safety of the home for the tree line once more. She kept to the outline of the property, unwilling to risk the light again.

There was little choice when she left the trees for the side of the garage. She skirted toward the back, but there was no entry point. The only door was in the front. Moving for the corner, Morgan reached out to take hold of the door handle. It wiggled, but remained locked. It wouldn't take much to gain entry if forced. However, the spotlight would not hesitate to showcase her efforts.

"Shit," Morgan quietly cursed. She took a series of quick breaths to work up her nerve. Jumping out in front of the door, Morgan slammed her shoulder above the lock. The door collapsed in just as the light triggered. Morgan dove inside. She whirled back, her hand forcing the door back into the frame. It refused to hold, but she kept it in place.

From outside, Morgan heard Kevin once more at the door. His muttering continued. They were the mumbles of the mentally disturbed, of a man as unhinged as the door in Morgan's hand.

She needed to be quick. The second the door shut behind him again, Morgan stood. The light continued to beam. Unfortunately, waiting wasn't an option any longer.

Turning from the door, Morgan used the outside light to see a narrow staircase. It led to the second floor. Her hand fell away from the door and she started up the steps.

The door at the top of the stairs was unlocked. Her hand, sweaty from her efforts, threatened to slip from the handle. Eventually, she found her grip and turned the knob until she heard the creak of the door swing into the room.

Morgan stepped into a bedroom. Every inch was decked out in pink and purple. Posters hung on the walls. Pictures of unicorns and rainbows filled the small desk in the corner. The entire place was a fantasy — a re-creation of former days.

Miriam lay chained in the corner. She stirred at Morgan's entry to the room. Her immediate retreat into the shadows made it clear Miriam was lost to panic at the thought of her captor's return.

"Hey," Morgan whispered. She lifted her hands before her. Noticing the gun still gripped tight, Morgan tucked the weapon away as she proceeded slowly across the dated carpet. "I'm not going to hurt you."

Miriam scrunched into a ball. Her hands covered her mouth. Tears ran over the tips of her fingers. They mixed with the snot flowing from her nose. She wore a glittery dress with ruffles. Even in the darkness, Morgan noticed the droplets of blood along one side. Bruises marked Miriam's face. There were cuts and scrapes on her arms.

"Miriam Prescott, right?" Morgan asked in a soft voice. "My name is Morgan. I'm here to help."

Her hands were slow to fall. Miriam was too afraid to believe in the new arrival, too scared to hope after what had happened to her. Morgan crept to the young woman's side, then crouched down to face her.

"I'm here to help."

Miriam looked her over. The panic receded. She pulled at the dress to cover herself up. "He made me wear this. He hurt me."

"I know," Morgan said. "But it's over now. Take my hand, and we—"

Miriam shook her head. She tucked low back into the corner. Her hands covered her once more. "No! No, no, no..."

"Miriam?" Morgan stood. Creaking filled the room. She was so focused on Miriam, Morgan forgot about the open door behind her.

Morgan spun. She drew her weapon as she faced the shadow in the center of the room. Before she steadied her aim toward Kevin, his hand swung wide. The blow caught her at the wrist and the gun sailed loose. It skittered across the carpet.

"What are you doing?" Kevin seethed. "She's mine!"

Morgan ducked the man's follow-up punch. A hand grabbed at the back of her leg. Miriam was crying for her, for the help and rescue promised by the DSA agent. The distraction was all Kevin needed to close in on Morgan.

"I finally have my sister back," he declared. Kevin grabbed Morgan by the shoulders. He pushed her hard to the side. Morgan's head slammed against the corner of the dresser.

"No one's taking her from me," the man railed. "No one!"

Dazed, Morgan swiped at the air to keep Kevin back. He swatted away her feeble attempts. Grabbing her by the hair, Kevin dragged her across the room. He lifted her up, the mania clear in his bulging eyes.

Then Morgan felt weightless. Her body soared from the room down the narrow staircase. The weightless sensation faded quickly as her body crashed along the steps on her way to the bottom. All breath left her as the darkness claimed her.

CHAPTER TWENTY-FIVE

Almost there...

The words repeated on Ben. They trailed his every thought. His eyes shifted to the clock again, constantly forgetting it no longer functioned in the van. Then they went for the watch he forgot to wear before falling on his phone. The small device sat on his lap. The screen lit up, yet carried no notification other than the slipping minutes. It was silent against the roar of the storm, both the one slamming against the windshield and the one banging around his head.

No word came from Morgan. She didn't answer his calls or respond to his texts. It had been almost an hour since the message about Kevin Drake. Even that had been the bare minimum: just a name and an address. There was only the quiet, and it unnerved him to no end.

They knew nothing of Morgan's situation. Ignorance was slowly becoming his standard operating procedure with the job. Something needed to change, and it started with Ben. He stewed in his silence, cursing his obsessive nature over the years of training that made him a decent cop. Preconceived notions clouded his judgment on everything—his desire to find Emily won out over common sense.

Now two lives were in danger. Miriam should have been the priority from the start. It took Ben far too long to figure that out. The delay put his partner at risk, and with each lost minute, he worried about what would be the ultimate cost of his selfishness.

Lizzy drove like a bat out of hell. The storm made visibility difficult, but the one saving grace was that the pounding rain forced people to stay home. Their absence gave them a clear path on the roads. They didn't need any obstacles to bar their progress. They had already created enough of them on their own.

Stray glances flew from Lizzy. Sadness and concern filled her wide green eyes. Both of them clearly regretted their decision to ignore Morgan.

"We'll get there," she whispered. Her foot pressed harder on the accelerator. The van rocked from the shift and the wheels kicked up a large puddle accumulated against the curb. "We will. We'll get there."

Doubt filled her voice. It was the first time Ben heard such a tone from the unflappable young woman. He reached for his phone, only to see no word from Morgan once again.

"We have to," he muttered. "We have to be there in time."

"It's not that far," Lizzy replied. She glanced at her own phone. The route lit up on the screen. They were still minutes from their destination.

The city fell away for the suburb of Andover. Still, they pushed on through the storm. The roads thinned, twisting around tall trees that swayed dangerously in the wind.

Ben beat his head against the seat. He felt every bump in the road, every subtle shift in the van. All rattled and shook him to the core. How many more times was he going to do this to Morgan? He had been a fool to leave her behind. She'd stuck with him through every false lead and every leap in judgment, all to aid him in his search for Emily.

"I need her to be alive," Ben said. "I need her to be alive so I can make this up to her."

Lizzy turned, a sad smile on her lips. She offered a slight nod, a clear acknowledgment of her own fault in the matter—not that Ben would ever let her take the blame. He had made a choice, and the consequences frightened him.

"She will be." The accelerator hit the floor; her boot threatened to push through the rusted-out base of the van. "We're almost there."

Ben took a breath. He cradled the silent phone, wishing for some sign of life from his partner. Then he tucked it away and leaned forward. His hands clasped in front of him, a prayer on his lips.

Almost there, Morgan. We're almost there.

CHAPTER TWENTY-SIX

Chains rattled along her wrists when Morgan stirred. Her head threatened to burst from the pain. Her body demanded to stay still, but she fought through the agony ripping through every muscle until she sat.

"That could have gone better," Morgan grumbled. The chains around her wrist confined her to the corner. She shook them loudly. The brace on the floor held firm. "Great."

"I'm sorry," a small voice rose from the other side of the bedroom. Morgan squinted to see Miriam cowering against the wall. Her glittery dress was the brightest thing in the room. "I didn't mean for that to happen, for him to hurt you, too."

"I know." Morgan shifted closer, fighting against her restraints. "I know you didn't, Miriam."

Miriam covered her eyes. Sobs rocked her body. "I mess up everything."

"Miriam, that's not..." Morgan stopped. She bit past her pain to throw on a smile. "Look at me, Miriam."

The young woman's head slowly rose. Morgan inched closer. "See? It's all right. *I'm* all right."

Miriam nodded. There was no hope in her eyes, no belief left in her. Kevin had beaten whatever remained from a life with an overbearing father and a pair of roommates who cared more about their appearance than helping their friend. Miriam remained alone in the world. Morgan needed her to look past that and recognize the truth of the situation — *their* situation.

"What did he say to you, Miriam?" Morgan asked. Her legs threatened to collapse beneath her, but she fought to stand. Morgan continued to creep closer to her companion. "What does he want?"

"He thinks I'm someone else," Miriam replied. "He doesn't even see me. No one does really, but he... he sees..."

"His sister," Morgan finished. Kevin's words echoed in her mind through the fog from the fall. *I finally have my sister back.*

"I'm going to die here, aren't I?" Miriam shook her head, afraid to take her eyes off the floor. "I've seen it in his face. He's going to figure out I'm not her eventually, and when he does, he's going to be so mad. He's going to... I'm going to die here in this terrible place, and no one is going to care."

"No," Morgan said. She crouched low. "Look at me, Miriam."

The young woman refused. She kept her eyes shut from the world, afraid to face reality.

"I need you to look at me, Miriam," Morgan repeated. "I need you to open your eyes."

"I don't want to," Miriam said. "Every time I try, he comes back."

"He's not here now." Morgan struggled to keep her voice steady. Her body wanted nothing more than to rest. Her head pounded for relief. Still, she kept her eyes on the cowering student. "It's natural to be scared, Miriam. I'm scared."

"Scared?" Miriam said through tears. "Try terrified!"

Morgan nodded. "I get it. I do. Being scared is natural. You're in a scary place, in an even scarier situation. That makes sense, and it's okay. But it's not okay to give up. Don't you dare give up on me, all right?"

Miriam wiped the tears and snot from her face. They ran in thin streams across her cheeks. "There's nothing we can do."

"That's not true."

"He'll hurt you," Miriam said. "He'll hurt you, then he'll... I don't want that."

"Neither do I," Morgan shot back. She tried to reach for Miriam, but the chains held her back. "I won't let him near you."

"You can't—"

"Look at me, Miriam." Morgan waited for Miriam to quiet the panic in her eyes. They washed over the agent. "I will not let that man near you again. Do you believe me?"

Miriam hesitated, then nodded. "Y... Yes."

The young woman's voice carried more strength than Morgan had noticed throughout their brief time together. Miriam needed to maintain that strength. It was the only thing that would see them through the night. That, and a little luck.

Morgan scanned the room. The door remained open to the stairs. It was a clear shot to the yard. If only they could break free from their chains. Morgan shifted back to the brace on the floor. The padlock was secured through the bar.

"I didn't notice a key." It was more to herself, yet her words carried across the room.

"I did," Miriam called. She crawled along the floor for the bed. Lifting the sheet, Miriam's hand dove beneath the mattress. When it returned, she held a small key in her hands.

"Where did you—"

"He dropped it when you were fighting. I was afraid, but I picked it up. Hid it before he noticed."

Morgan held out her hands. "His mistake. And our good fortune."

Miriam tossed the key. Morgan snatched it from the air. An enthused chuckle fell from her lips as she darted toward the padlock. The lock opened, and the chains slipped from her wrists to the floor.

"Time to get out of here, Miriam," Morgan said. Quick steps carried the agent over to the wounded woman. The chains rattled loose. Morgan stood and held out a hand to her companion. "You with me?"

Miriam took Morgan's hand. She gripped it tight, a lifeline to freedom. Morgan wasn't about to let her go.

"Good girl."

CHAPTER TWENTY-SEVEN

"Stay close to me."

Morgan led the way down the stairs. Miriam continued to hold tight to her hand. Bare feet rushed along in tune to Morgan's own hurried steps. The door at the base continued to fight against the wind outside, beating against the frame.

They stopped shy of the door. Rain poured from the sky in massive waves. The crack of thunder rumbled much too closely, and lightning scraped the sky seconds after.

The house was dark. Morgan didn't know how much time had passed since her fall, how much time she'd wasted in unconsciousness. Needless to say, it appeared Kevin had retired for the night. Their luck continued.

Miriam squeezed Morgan's hand. She patted along the woman's back. "We need to go."

Morgan sensed the woman's unease. Miriam's fear was returning, the brief glimmer of bravery an illusion that cracked the longer they waited to escape.

"I know," Morgan said. "But first we need to—"

"No," Miriam said over the agent. "I have to get out of here before he comes back. Before—"

She pushed through Morgan. Her hand dropped away. Morgan tried to grab for her, but Miriam was already outside. The damage was done in an instant, and their luck vanished.

The spotlight kicked on, shining down upon Miriam. It was the brightest light either had seen in some time, the effects blinding and debilitating. The unseen effect drove Miriam's fear into overdrive.

"Oh, no," the young woman whispered. She ran toward the

driveway, the opposite of where Morgan wanted to lead her companion.

"Dammit." Morgan bolted from the garage. Blinking rapidly, her eyes adjusted to the spotlight above. She snatched Miriam's arm to take the lead once more. It was too late to pull her back to the shadows of the yard and the tree line beyond. There wasn't time to backtrack. The damage caused by the light was done. Instead, Morgan continued down the driveway, pulling the young woman through the rain.

They rounded the corner to the home, the street in the distance, but finally within view. Freedom was in their grasp.

The side door to the home opened. Hope left them. All thought of freedom went silent. Kevin stepped out into the rain. Morgan's sidearm was at his side, his finger poised against the trigger.

"Oh, God." Miriam clutched tight to Morgan's side. Her body threatened to give way to her cowardice—to the hopelessness that turned her into a whimpering child.

Morgan held her up, refusing to let fear win out over her. "It's okay, Miriam. It's going to be okay."

"It's not," Kevin yelled from a distance. "You think you can take her from me? She's my sister!"

Miriam's body rocked with growing sobs. "It's going to happen again. He's going to hurt me and lock me away."

Morgan turned to the young woman. She grabbed both of Miriam's arms and squeezed. Rain washed over her face and both had to squint to view anything through the storm. "He's not going to hurt you again. You have to believe that. You have to find the strength to never back down from the devils of the world. Not for an instant."

Morgan's hands fell away. She didn't bother to wait for a sign that the young woman understood. Words only carried so much weight. In the end, actions were required to win the day, and it fell to Morgan to show the young woman the way.

The second Morgan let go of Miriam, she turned toward Kevin and broke into a run. She blitzed at the armed man. The sudden assault shocked him, his reaction slow to respond. Morgan didn't let up, racing for Kevin with everything she had left. She pushed through the pain of their previous struggle, and her own gnawing fear of facing the end of her story without Ben by her side.

"I'll kill you," Kevin seethed. "I swear I will."

"Go ahead and try."

No matter her speed, and no matter the delay in his reaction, the distance was too great to cover. Kevin raised the sidearm and fired. Morgan felt the bullet whip by her right arm, the shot wide by a hair's breadth.

There was no time for a second shot. Morgan was in front of him, her fist flying. It collided with his chin. The impact whipped his head back and drove him away from her.

The gun remained in play. Morgan used the momentary jolt from her first blow to leap at the weapon. Her nails dug into his flesh. Kevin screamed. The pain caused his fingers to loosen. The gun slipped free and clattered to their feet.

Morgan bent to reach for the weapon. Kevin was too quick, however. He snatched her arm and threw her against the house.

Kevin scrambled for the gun. "You can't have her. I won't let you take her from me."

"She isn't your sister." Morgan pushed from the house. As Kevin bent for the gun, Morgan brought up her knee. It slammed into his cheek, upending him until he crashed to the ground. Morgan kicked at the pavement; the gun skidded across the driveway. "You have to know that on some level, Kevin."

"She's just being bad," Kevin said. Fighting for his feet, he wiped away the blood on his lips. "Dad always taught me how to stop from being bad."

"By hurting her," Morgan said. "Like he hurt you."

"It was the only way!" the man-child raged.

"You think strength is a hefty bicep and a powerful swing." She shook her head. "It's not. It's the resolve to never surrender your principles."

Kevin barreled toward Morgan. Nothing would stand in his way. Morgan felt the same way. When he reached her, Morgan stepped aside. She brought her fist down on his cheek once more. The blow drove him to the pavement, where he collapsed in a heap.

"Never," she said. Her words carried on the wind toward her companion. Miriam looked on in surprise, her hands over her lips.

"Morgan!" The shout came from the street. In the flurry of

the fight, Morgan never even noticed the headlamps from the rusty van parked across the way. Ben ran across the lawn, not letting up until he reached her. Arms pulled her close in a tight hug.

Morgan laughed. "About time you showed up."

"Not that you needed the help." Ben let her go. His hand grazed her cheek, concern welling in his eyes. "Are you—"

Her head demanded relief. Her body suffered from the fall, and if she didn't completely focus, there were three Bens standing before her. None of that stopped her. "I'm good," she said. "Feeling much better now."

Miriam slowly approached. Morgan reached out to the young woman. "You all right, Miriam?"

"I—" Her eyes widened. "Look out!"

Kevin was on his feet. Morgan's gun was in his hands. He took aim at Miriam. "I loved you so much."

"Kevin, don't!" Morgan shouted. She was too far from Miriam to save her, and too far from Kevin to stop him.

"Hey, Kevin," a voice called out. Kevin turned to see Lizzy raise her camera to greet him. "Say cheese."

The flash filled the driveway. Kevin reeled back, a hand over his face. "I can't see!"

"That's probably best for what's coming," Ben remarked with a wince.

"Huh?" Kevin dropped his hand from his eyes.

Miriam's fist cocked back, then shot out. Every ounce of strength, every swallowed bit of rage and anger over her abduction, joined her in one sweeping blow. Cartilage crunched under her striking fist as Kevin's nose broke. The gun sailed free, and Kevin staggered back. His body crashed against the side of his house. Siding shattered and showered over him as he fell to the pavement and, this time, failed to get back up.

CHAPTER TWENTY-EIGHT

The hum of the road accompanied Adler's swirling thoughts as she stared out the passenger side window. The cool night air slammed against the vehicle. Kanigher kept a firm hand on the steering wheel, steadying them in the center of their lane. Traffic blurred by them; bright headlights shifted to red taillights in a stream.

They were in no rush. Adler saw to that. She had kept them at the diner for well over two hours after Zac's departure. She'd wanted to go after him, to make him see the truth behind her need for his return to the DSA. Kanigher had been the voice of reason on the subject. He had given Zac time to come back without complaint, though she had seen how tired her companion had grown over the course of their long day.

Eventually, though, Adler knew it had been time to leave. The temperatures had dropped considerably. Rain was in the offering, and she wanted to get home before the storm set in. They headed east for the airport, the quiet between them settling in like an old friend.

"We're all set," Adler said to fill the void. "Our red-eye takes off in three hours."

"Plenty of time." Kanigher kept his eyes on the road. She was grateful to have him with her, always mindful and always considerate. "Need anything?"

She needed Zac. Not just for a damn signal that seemed to elude all her attempts to trace, but to figure out what was wrong with the man. Zac was sick, visibly falling apart, yet said nothing during their conversation. He had refused to reach out for a helping hand, even with one thrown at him. Why? What secret was he hiding now, and how would it come back to haunt them in the end?

Kanigher glanced over, and she caught his concern in the reflection of the passenger-side window. "Not how you wanted things to turn out today?"

She smirked at his summation. Turning away from the open road out her window, Adler settled against the seat and let out a long breath. "I thought I was doing the right thing trying to bring Zac home," she said. "I hated how we abandoned him, regretted the secrets kept for so long when he was working for Sullivan. I don't know. He lost so much. I thought I could give him something back."

Kanigher gave a slight nod. His hand tightened on the wheel. "Some people don't want a helping hand. Even when they're standing at the edge of the cliff."

"Or when they're already falling," Adler remarked. Zac had been nervous, sweating, and clearly off. The weight loss alone had been a chief indicator of his state. Coupled with his anger and behavior in the diner, she realized more brewed within her old colleague. "Something else was going on. There's something wrong with Zac."

"I've said so from the beginning," Kanigher replied. "I didn't have extensive contact with him while I was at the NSA, but there were a few occasions where I had to deal with the man. Modine always struck me as self-important. Pretentious to a fault. Truth is, you've outshined him on every level."

"Me? No way."

Kanigher shrugged. His full attention returned to the road. The silence fell between them, filling the cabin of the vehicle. From the distance, storm clouds swept across the sky. Adler watched them rise like a giant wave.

She refused to let Kanigher be right about her. She hadn't been placed in Zac's department to outshine him. Metcalf had placed Adler in Operations to spy on Zac, to monitor his communications and report back. She had been a buffer, hampering Zac's efforts, while also creating a stopgap in case his duplicity went too far.

Her very presence had sent Zac spiraling. By sending Adler in the room with him, he had gone running to Sullivan's side in retaliation. His poor choices had resulted from her arrival, and it weighed on her greatly.

"It's about that signal, isn't it?" Kanigher asked. She turned to him, confused. "You think he would have found it by now?"

"I know he would have," she said. Her gaze fell, her hands clasped tight in her lap. "No, it's more than that. Zac always held things together. He was the glue that kept the DSA whole."

"I don't know —"

"Things only went wrong when Zac and Metcalf fell apart," Adler continued. "His work in the Operations Room kept the field team in the loop at all times, right alongside the research team. He held it all together. Just him."

"And you can't?"

She shook her head. "I'm not that person. Never have been."

Kanigher offered her a smirk. "You're stronger than you give yourself credit for. You'll see."

She didn't think so. Nothing in her past made her feel strong. There was nothing from her time in the field, or at the office, that gave her the confidence to coordinate their efforts against the growing forces against them. Not with a threat like the Trust, or the mysterious signal that ate up her every stray thought.

Adler returned to the window and the night outside. She wanted the shadows to swallow her whole. She hoped the darkness would open up and reveal the secrets hidden inside.

"What was he hiding, Kanigher?"

"Everyone has something to hide," Kanigher said. "He'll handle it his way, Alison. That's how he wanted it. It was his choice. Remember that."

The car left the thruway for a rest stop. A fluorescent sign at the end of the short ramp beckoned them to its waiting parking lot. Kanigher circled the lot, driving past the gas station for the convenience store in the back. He parked on the side and turned off the engine.

"Snack break," he announced. "It's no risotto, but it will have to do. Want anything?"

Adler offered a sad smile. "Surprise me."

"Challenge accepted," he said with a wink. He slipped out of the car and headed inside.

Adler was left with nothing but her thoughts in the darkness. Worry continued to plague her. Something was wrong with Zac, something she had triggered with her mention of the signal.

"What are you hiding, Zac?" she said to the shadows. "And why do I get the feeling it's going to come back to haunt us in the end?"

CHAPTER TWENTY-NINE

Kanigher wandered the aisles of the convenience store. He grabbed a pair of Hostess pies from the end cap, then headed for the refrigerator units at the back. He scanned the limited selection. The truck must have skipped a delivery or ten from the looks of things. Resigned between a six-pack of root beer and a two-liter of RC Cola, Kanigher grabbed the root beer from the fridge.

The clerk offered a nod at Kanigher's approach. He turned away from the television—another late-night reality show Kanigher had never heard of—and rang up the goods.

"Pack of smokes or lottery tickets?" the clerk asked with no emotion. He threw in an uneven smile that showed off the yellow of his teeth.

"Pass," Kanigher replied. "I'm not that lucky."

"You never know."

Kanigher shook his head. "Unfortunately, I do."

Today was a clear indication of that much. There was still no word from Metcalf about her secret operation with Nixon. On top of that, a Hostess pie now replaced what should have been a delicious risotto. A lesson about not admitting boredom fit somewhere in the events of his day, but Kanigher tried his best to ignore it.

Collecting his sugar fix, Kanigher headed outside. The cool breeze whipped at him and caused the door to swing rapidly back in its frame. Kanigher threw an innocent wave at the startled clerk, who went back to watching his show.

Adler still stared out the window. The day hadn't gone well for either of them. Out of the two, she bore the brunt of the disappointment. The weight of the entire DSA sat on her slumped shoulders and caused a crease above her brow. The job was aging her already, sucking the innocence away from her.

Kanigher hated to see it. He wanted to help her, but when it came to computers, there was no hope for him. The scientific aspects of the job always remained out of reach. He was a man of action. Strap a gun on his hip and a Kevlar vest on his chest, and he was ready to face anything the world tossed his way.

That wasn't the way Adler was wired. She was thoughtful and kind, two traits not typically seen in the world of intelligence and espionage. He was honest with her about her strength. He recognized it within her. If only she would take a step back to see it for herself.

Unfortunately, she couldn't see anything at the moment. Blinders and limitations held her in place—her own doing—and it would take time for her to push through them. He knew she could, though; she could pull the team together and even crack this issue with the rogue signal. All she needed to do was open her eyes to her true potential.

That wasn't the only thing she failed to see in the shadows of the long night. Kanigher picked them up from across the median on the interstate. Three black SUVs in a caravan headed toward Arcadia. Tinted windows hid their occupants from view, but Kanigher didn't need to see them to know who they were... and who they were after.

"Better hurry," Adler called. Her words drew his attention from the street. When he looked back, the SUVs were out of sight. They would reach Arcadia within the hour. "Kanigher?"

"I'm coming."

"The wind is picking up," Adler said. "Storm will be here soon."

Kanigher tossed her a nod, followed by her Hostess pie. "Just give me a minute, and we'll get moving."

He set the root beer on his seat. The pie was about to join it, but then he caught Adler eyeing the snack up. He kept the pie close, stepping away from the car as he opened it up for a bite.

No more SUVs followed the caravan. There were no other indicators of trouble. Yet, Kanigher knew three would be enough. There was every chance he was wrong, but he certainly didn't think so, not after seeing Zac in Arcadia.

Zac, however, was on his own. That was the way he wanted it, and Kanigher was more than content to keep his problems as far away from the DSA as possible. They had their own troubles on the horizon.

The first drops of rain tapped along the roof of the rental car. They came slow and sporadic, but quickened with each rolling cloud. Kanigher rushed for the car. He slipped inside as the sky opened up.

"Told you," Adler said, her mouth full of her pie.

Kanigher quickly rolled up the window to cut off the rain. He set the pie on his lap and backed the car out of the parking spot.

A storm was coming, all right. Kanigher only hoped Zac had as much sense to realize it before the storm found him.

CHAPTER THIRTY

Flashing lights filled the road. Patrol cars parked on the front lawn and along the neighbors' property on both sides. Officers cordoned off the scene, while forensics raced around the far side of the home for the two-story garage in the back. The case may have been solved, and the girl saved, but the cleanup had only begun.

Kevin stumbled down the driveway. Two officers held him up. His hands were strapped in cuffs in front of him. They tossed him in the back of a patrol car and secured the door. His swollen eyes stared back at Miriam, the confusion still written all over his face.

Miriam's hands continued to shake from the affair. Her body trembled, and she flinched at every sudden movement toward her. Recovery would be slow, but it would come in time.

She sat beside Morgan as they were checked over by the EMT. A bandage covered most of Morgan's forehead. The light still caused her to wince when shone directly in her face. Cuts and bruises dotted Miriam's arms and legs, her ordeal more pro-longed than Morgan's.

Ben paced the other side of the driveway. His own frustration at what had happened refused to abate. He should have been with Morgan the entire time. There was every chance none of her injuries would have come to pass, and Miriam would have been saved that much sooner.

He tried to let it go, to see the positive in the situation. Every attempt met with more self-recriminations when Morgan glanced his way.

"Sir, do you mind?" the EMT asked.

Ben stopped his pacing. All three stared at him, the glower from Morgan the most telling. "What?"

"Your pacing is freaking the man out, Riley," Morgan said. She held the bandage to her head, sucking in air with the slightest touch. "Walk it off."

"I could help," Ben started. All three shook their heads at once. "Or I could walk it off."

"There you go," Morgan said.

"That would be best," the EMT continued.

Even Miriam agreed. "Thank you."

Ben huffed. He jammed his hands into his pockets, then started for the street. He paused as another cruiser cut a swath through the myriad vehicles already present and parked in the driveway. His hand shot up to cover his eyes, the light from the headlamps almost blinding in their intensity.

Bellamy jumped out of the car. His heavy boots stomped along the asphalt. "Dunleavy?"

"Right here, Bellamy," Morgan called with a raised hand to flag him down. Bellamy halted just shy of the EMT and his patients, panic on his face.

"Are you—" he asked, trying to catch his breath. "Is she... Is that—"

"Miriam Prescott."

Bellamy's hands fell to his hips. He let out a long breath; relief escaped into the air. Reaching into his pocket, Bellamy pulled out a single sheet of paper. "I found your note at the command post. I can't believe you went off on your own like that! You—"

"I got her, Bellamy," Morgan interrupted. She stood and her hand settled on his shoulder. "She's safe. It's over."

Bellamy removed his hat and ran his hand along his brow. "I should have listened to you."

"The trail in the forest?"

"Dumbass kids," Bellamy replied. "Stupid frat boys sent a group of pledges in for the night as punishment. Just dumb luck Miriam was taken from the spot they entered the woods."

Ben left Morgan with Bellamy, who continued to apologize for his behavior. Ben's own efforts fell short and his guilt followed him all the way to the street.

Lizzy sat on the back of her van. She looked too innocent, and way too young, for the sadness that sat in her eyes. Sipping some coffee, the photographer stared off into the distance, lost to the night. Ben took the seat next to her.

Lizzy held out the coffee. Ben shook his head. Caffeine was the last thing he needed. A strawberry-mango smoothie would have been appreciated, though.

"She was right," Lizzy said, unable to look at him. She dumped out the remnants of her drink, then crushed the paper cup. "Your partner."

Ben shook his head. "She was, but... I was wrong to say those things to you before."

"Nay. I needed to hear them, and you needed to say them."

Ben sighed. His hands settled on the bumper for support. "There was no grand conspiracy here. Just a man who had lost his sister."

Lizzy nodded. "When she went missing three years ago."

Ben's brow furrowed.

Lizzy pointed inside the van and the network running a search. "She had been walking down the street to the local market. That was the last time anyone ever saw her. Police never found her."

The young woman jumped down from the van. More sat on the tip of her tongue. Ben intervened before she could speak.

"It's terrible, Lizzy, but it happens," Ben said. "It doesn't mean the two events are connected."

Lizzy squeezed her fists tighter, then let them fall. Her hand lifted the ball cap from her head, and she ran her fingers through her thick hair. "Right."

"What is it?"

"They just..." Lizzy stopped and put her hat back on. She leaned along the bumper of the car. Her eyes met Ben's. "I heard over the radio that Miriam's father is no longer running for City Council in the fall. Wonder what might have changed his mind?"

She pushed from the bumper and started for the driver's-side door. Ben pursued, his eyes wide in surprise. "You can't possibly think—"

"I can," she said.

Ben spun her around. "Kevin Drake was mentally ill, not some mass manipulator."

Lizzy pulled away from him. "Who lives fifteen miles from campus, yet somehow found his way to Miriam Prescott."

"There could be any number of reasons for that."

A chuckle slipped from her lips. She wiped them clean and nodded. "You're right." Sad eyes pulled him in. "Some of us have to find the right one. I get it. You don't believe me. I'm used to it. Doesn't mean I'll stop. I'll just have to believe for both of us, Ben."

Lizzy opened the door and slipped inside. It closed behind her.

"Liz, wait."

She stuck her head out the window. Her smile was back, so confident and assured. "I won't stop, Ben. I won't stop looking for the Emily Wrights of the world."

There was no talking her down, and even less of a reason to try. Lizzy saw the world in her own way, and who was to say she wasn't right, at least on some level.

"I won't argue the point." His hand settled over hers. "I only hope you're right."

"I am," Lizzy said. "You'll see."

His hand fell away, and he took a step from the van. "Take care of yourself."

"I'm the only one who will," Lizzy said. She tossed him a sarcastic salute. "Be seeing you, Agent."

Ben headed back to the crime scene. Halfway across the street, he took one last look at Lizzy and her rusted-out van. He worried for her future. The journey ahead was not one he envied, but she had questions that needed answering.

No one was going to stop her from finding them.

CHAPTER THIRTY-ONE

Lizzy settled into the driver's seat of the van. She looked over to the passenger side, only to see emptiness. A solemn smile escaped her. It was nice to have someone by her side for a change, someone who believed in the work. Even with the way things ended, knowing the doubts Ben held for her theories, Lizzy remained hopeful for the future.

There wasn't any need to carry things further with Ben. They had saved Miriam and caught a bad guy. Lizzy remained wary of the outcome, but let it rest with her federal friends—if that's what they truly were. She never found out the truth about them.

That was all right. Everyone needed their secrets. Lizzy sure had plenty to spare over the course of her investigations, and rather than argue with Ben—or God forbid Morgan—Lizzy kept them inside. It was easier for everyone that way.

The connections hidden beneath the surface were there, but only she could see them. Ben and Morgan weren't to blame, any more than Miriam was for what happened to her. Lizzy was alone in this fight and always would be.

Miriam was targeted for a reason, and it went beyond her similar physical appearance to Kevin Drake's sister. Kevin's involvement alone sparked a debate in her mind. He might have been local, but he'd never been to the university before. It was in the opposite direction of his place of employment. Nothing suggested any sort of visit to the campus before, yet somehow he had known exactly where to find Miriam for her nightly jog.

That fact was not alone in its impracticality. There was also Daryl Fletcher. If Ben heard the name again, he would have screamed at her, but she couldn't let the man go. Fletcher had made a comment about praying for Miriam to them in the aftermath of their unfortunate break-in. He'd even made the Sign of the Cross.

But he had done so with his left hand. Ben had failed to notice, but Lizzy had picked up on it immediately. The sign was always made with the right hand. Any practicing Catholic would know that much. Fletcher, however, was anything but. He was a known agnostic, who used his faithlessness as the subject of many lectures in the past.

Lizzy didn't press the issue, but merely sought to understand the connections laid out before her. Miriam Prescott. Daryl Fletcher. Even Miriam's father had played a part in tonight's drama by stepping down from a competitive City Council position. A wider picture came into focus for Lizzy, one no one else picked up on or bothered to identify. They had come to save a missing girl and had done so.

The rest was up to Lizzy. It would always be up to her.

Her phone buzzed along the dash. Lizzy grabbed it, the vibrations almost causing her to drop the small device. She noted Hector's image on the display before she answered the call.

"I didn't think you'd pick up," Hector said through the speaker.

She shifted the phone between her ear and shoulder to pin it in place. Then she let the van roar to life. "Thought about ignoring it."

"I figured."

"What can I do for you, Hector?"

Hector sighed. He clearly didn't want an argument either tonight. "When are you heading home again?"

"I'm not sure. I—"

"I thought we might grab some dinner," Hector said over her. They both knew the answer. That wasn't the purpose of the call. "I didn't like how things ended, and wanted a chance to talk things out."

It was the closest to an apology she'd ever heard from the man. Unfortunately, she also knew what came attached to the meal: another lecture.

"I'll be home when I can."

"Lizzy, you can't keep—"

Her phone chirped. She pulled the device from her ear, turning the call to speaker before checking the latest notification.

"You're not listening to me anymore, are you?"

"Of course I am." Lizzy flipped through the alert. Another person was missing, another soul that needed rescuing.

"No, you're not," Hector said with a sigh. "There was a break in the speaker. Meaning you just got another case."

"It's closer to home," Lizzy said. "Utah." She could be there by midday if she drove through the night. Lizzy set the phone on the dash, then rubbed at her eyes. Any exhaustion felt from her time in Wichita vanished. She buried it, along with any doubts and recriminations associated with the last couple of days. Someone needed her. Too many people needed her.

"Would it help if I asked you to be careful?" Hector asked.

"Couldn't hurt," Lizzy said. "Hector, I—"

"I know," he said with concern in his voice. "You have to do this. I understand."

"I'll talk to you soon." She ended the call and let the navigation app take over. Turning back for a moment, Lizzy took one last look at the crowd of officials and smiled. Miriam was safe. It was time to save someone else.

There was a reason behind the missing, a purpose to their disappearances. Lizzy Doyle was sure as hell going to find it.

CHAPTER THIRTY-TWO

Morgan found Ben standing in the center of the street. His hair was matted down, his clothes dripping wet in the storm's aftermath. Heavy shoulders and a soulful stare revealed the sadness he carried. His gaze trailed the departing van.

Lizzy was out of their lives. Morgan listed it as a blessing, but her departure came with a whole new set of worries. She wondered if letting someone like Lizzy out in the world was for the best, or if they should have done more to curb her investigative tendencies.

There was also her conspiratorial nature to consider. Ben believed, though the doubts clearly seeped through over the course of their time together. Belief was all Ben had in his life: that Emily was still alive, that they would come through the other side of things okay.

Morgan held no such belief. Her own hope came not in lofty ideals, but in the man she kept at her side. She believed in people, Ben most of all. She simply wished he saw things the same.

Shifting through the parking lot of police cars, Morgan joined her partner. Her hand came to rest on his shoulder. The touch snapped him out of his daze. When he turned toward her, he offered a lackluster smile.

Ben looked her over, the smile quickly fading. Her head pounded, the pain visible to her worried partner. It was the cost of doing business in their line of work, and she wouldn't exchange it for anything, especially considering the results of their evening.

Miriam continued to be treated by the EMT. The technician joked with the college girl, the man's bedside manner doing more to help Miriam than any bandage or antiseptic could.

"Think she's going to be all right?" Ben asked.

"She will," Morgan replied. Miriam caught them looking. She threw them a slight wave, which they reciprocated before moving out of sight. "It's you I'm concerned about."

Ben sighed. "I made a mess of this, didn't I?"

"Pretty big one, yes."

"I'm sorry, Morgan." He shook his head, fighting back a scream of frustration. "I let my need to find Emily cloud my judgment."

"Yeah, well, I should have been more understanding and less—"

"Morgan-like?"

Morgan punched his arm lightly. "Watch it."

Ben staggered a step from the playful blow. The grin returned to his face, this time genuine and light. She loved it most about him, and his smile brought one to her own lips.

"Ben—"

"I know, Morgan," he said. "I haven't been on the same page with you for a while. I have to be better."

"You do," she shot back. "You ran off on your own to play hero, not caring about what I would have wanted. Then there was that crap with Wesley Fuller. You wrote him off right out of the gate because you were too caught up in your own fight with the Trust. I thought you had some sense of things after that, but to do it again with Miriam?"

Ben huffed. Every word hit him, the impact clear in his tired eyes. He moved for the closest vehicle and leaned against the side. "Guess almost dying messed me up more than I thought."

"You think?"

Ben's gaze thinned. "I get it, Morgan. You were right. You're always right."

She joined him on the side of the car. "Much as I love to hear it, that's not what this is about."

"I'm trying, Morgan. I am."

"It's not just about you, Ben," she said. "It's about us."

"I feel a lecture coming on."

"Stop," she said with a raised finger. She pushed from the car and moved in front of him. He turned away. Her hand fell on his chin to lift him back to her. "Stop with the jokes."

Ben took a deep breath. Quiet settled over them.

"We're stronger together, Ben," she started. "There are too many wolves at the door, too many monsters in the dark, waiting to take us apart."

"I'm aware," Ben said. "I'm trying to—"

"Not done, partner," Morgan interrupted. "We might have our backs against the wall, but I am here for you. I am not going anywhere. Whatever mistakes you think you've made, or that I've thrown at you—"

"Which is quite a few, by the way."

"I'm still here, is what I'm saying," Morgan said. "And I'm trying to say that we will find her, Ben. Emily may be one of the missing, but it won't be forever. Because she has you watching out for her, there will always be hope."

Ben settled against the car. The argument on his lips fell. Morgan took a step back to give him room, to let their words sink in completely.

He nodded. "Thanks, partner."

"Don't mention it." The pair left the comfort of the car for the street ahead. It was a walk to the rental car. They kept their pace slow. The chill wind left by the storm pushed them along.

"I won't, if you won't tell the others how absolutely useless I was in taking down Drake."

Morgan laughed, the sound filling the road. "Oh, I'm telling them. Every detail."

"Come on, Morgan."

"I might even add some flourishes along the way," she said, a spring in her step as she quickened toward the car. "Weren't you crying the whole time?"

"That's..." Ben shook his head. "That's not even funny."

"Then why am I laughing?"

"You're terrible, lady. Absolutely terrible." Ben put his arm around her to pull her close. "I'm glad you're all right."

They were both going to be all right. The conflict within would remain, of course. His obsession versus the fight of the day would always cause rifts between them. But she would always be there to pull him back. He gave her hope and she could do no less.

"Let's go home, partner."

CHAPTER THIRTY-THREE

"I should have known you were behind this, Hollis," Metcalf said. Men surrounded her at the elevator. One patted her down for weaponry. The USB was seized by another during the search, and an inquisitive look passed to the man behind the curtain. A slight nod offered the bodyguard his answer. He smashed the drive beneath his boot.

"As I should have had more faith that Susan Metcalf would never meet her end in a mundane traffic accident." Hollis' grin never wavered. He clearly enjoyed every second of this. He stepped aside, showcasing the empty table to the left.

A hand escorted Metcalf by her elbow. She glanced up at the sight of General Adams in a tight button-down with a blazer over it. "I see your recent defection with Sullivan hasn't hurt your standing with this crowd, Thomas."

Adams tossed her to her seat. She gripped the sides tight to steady herself, the smile ever present on her face.

Metcalf tilted her head after Adams, who retreated deeper into the crowd. "Still a little sensitive over the matter?"

Hollis fixed his collar and cleared his throat, then took the seat across from her. "Let's just say he's learned a hard lesson, as has his son."

Metcalf trailed Hollis' gaze to the younger Adams. He huddled in the corner, barely able to look in their direction. His face was a massive bruise, and a splint held three broken fingers in place on his right hand.

"Who knew you could be so forgiving?" Metcalf said. "Of course, it would be difficult to replace a four-star general in your ranks, not to mention the resources at his son's disposal, wouldn't it?"

"Not as difficult as you would imagine," Hollis replied smugly.

Silence continued to rule the rest of the penthouse. All eyes were on their exchange. Metcalf took a second to scan each turned head for recognition. There were high-profile members of the intelligence community side by side with Hollywood's best and brightest. She recognized several political insiders, like Malcolm Richards, standing among bigwigs in the pharmaceutical industry, like Marybeth Black. All co-mingled, living their lavish lives with no concern for anyone they deemed beneath them.

Hollis snapped his fingers. In an instant, the music resumed, and the conversations picked back up. Their table was forgotten, invisible to the festivities surrounding them.

"Cute trick."

"A drink, my dear?" Hollis asked. She gave away nothing, settling back in her chair. Hollis' gaze fell. "Right. The stoic politician returns. I would have thought those days behind you after everything."

"You mean everything you caused?" Metcalf said. "Sullivan was working for you the entire time. You: the man behind the Trust."

"Sullivan..." Hollis paused. He finished his glass of champagne. "Sullivan was a mistake. Then again, we all make mistakes, don't we, Susan? Surely you recognize yours now."

Metcalf chuckled. She leaned closer, her hands poised on the table. "I'm right where I want to be."

She glanced around again. This was the Trust. For months, there had been nothing but rumors and innuendo. She, herself, believed their very existence an impossibility given her history. Now she knew, without a shadow of a doubt, they were real. Her fight held merit, and she was ready as hell to see it through.

Hollis read her cold stare. He leaned over the table, elbows on the surface. "Because I allowed it," he replied with his patented smirk in place. "I've very much been aware of your pathetic DSA's effort to learn about our organization. I simply afforded you the opportunity."

"You're a showman, Hollis," she said with the shake of her head. "A good one, true, but I don't buy it. Eventually, they won't either."

"These fine folk?" Hollis projected his voice to draw eyes back to him. "These are *my* people. Let me show you."

He snapped his fingers again. Two guards shuffled from the back of the room, a man caught between their arms. It was St. James, the cereal mogul.

Metcalf and her team had learned of his involvement with the DSA the previous week while recruiting Nixon to their cause. They had left the man unconscious in the street, a ruse to scare him enough to make a mistake. His connection with Duloc had brought her to the hotel.

Hollis had been telling the truth: this conversation was his doing.

"I believe you already know Mr. St. James, don't you?" Hollis stood and circled behind the cringing mogul.

"David, listen—" St. James pleaded.

Hollis' hands fell on the man's shoulders. The two guards took a step back, yet remained within reach of their boss.

"St. James here made a... well, let's call it an error in judgment," Hollis said. "He took your message to heart and completely forgot who his friends were. How despite all the nasty, false information about his business dealings that made it out into the world, he could have come to me—to us—and we would have helped him. Quietly."

"David, I didn't—"

"Instead," Hollis said, gripping the man's shoulders tighter. "He broke protocol and leaked more intel in an effort to save his own skin."

"Hollis," Metcalf called. "You don't have to do this."

"I'm not doing anything, Susan." His smirk was back—that pretentious mask he wore to hide his vindictive nature. She had seen it in his interviews with his team at the DSA. She had even seen it before then, during multiple dealings with the Inter-Agency Council. Hollis was a snake, waiting to make his kill. "Mr. St. James understood the rules, and he broke them."

"David, I... I can make this right," St. James said. Sweat poured down his cheeks. "I can fix this."

"We *are* fixing it, my friend," Hollis whispered into the man's ears. He pushed off the man's shoulders, which forced St. James to the ground. Hollis held out a hand, and the guard to his right passed over his sidearm.

"Hollis, don't!"

The gun boomed throughout the penthouse. St. James did not get up. Blood pooled from the headshot, a puddle streaming out from around his bulbous frame.

Hollis handed the gun back to his guard, then fixed his jacket. He let out a long, calm breath before retaking his seat at the table. Any argument over what was just witnessed by the crowd, any misgivings at all at the death of a man most in the room probably called friend or more, was lost to the music echoing off the walls of the penthouse.

Another snap of the fingers, and the guards removed the dead from sight. The party resumed, as if nothing had happened.

"You see, Susan, this is the Trust," Hollis said. "I am the Trust in every way, shape, and form. I have set these people up for life and handed them the future."

Metcalf wanted to scream. A man was killed to set an example, and to push her to act. She bit the inside of her cheek. "A future offered by the Wellspring. With tech she created."

"Created, sure," Hollis said, resting comfortably in his chair. "But it was the people in this room who fully developed and distributed that technology."

Metcalf nodded. "You control it."

Hollis' eyes thinned. "Humanity is at a tipping point. Move too quickly or stray from the path set and chaos rules."

"What's at the end of your so-called path?"

Excitement grew in Hollis' face, wide eyes and a wider smile. "That, my dear Susan, is exactly what I find myself asking more and more. And the very subject we were set to discuss when you so rudely barged in."

"Care to share your conclusions?"

Hollis wagged his finger. "I think not. You've proven poor company, Susan. I'm sorry you won't be able to witness our grand utopia."

"Don't be." Metcalf removed her left earring and held it between her fingers. "Neither will you."

"What are you—"

She snapped the earring in two, cutting the electronic circuit within the small innocuous piece of jewelry. In the blink of an eye, the lighting in the penthouse went out. Nixon had received her signal and acted accordingly.

"The lights!" a guard shouted.

Metcalf leaped from her chair. The guard's cry immediately gave away his position. Metcalf rushed at him. She slid to his side, then kicked out to cut him down at the knees. The man dropped, crying out. She was on top of him in an instant. A solid punch to his glass jaw sent him to dreamland with minimal resistance. With his gun in hand, Metcalf made it back to her feet.

"Where is she?" Hollis snarled.

Shadows blurred as panic set in throughout the penthouse. Partygoers screamed in terror, their night ruined by the darkness and the sudden violence erupting around them. They dashed for the stairs and the elevators, trampling over all in their way.

Metcalf used the chaos to her advantage. With a weapon in hand, she fired at the guards. Three fell from her barrage.

Hollis was on the move before she could take him out. "Get her, you fools!"

Metcalf unloaded her clip at the man in the pale suit. Hollis dove under the hail of gunfire. He crashed along the tile and slid into the open elevator doors.

Four men followed, surrounding him as Hollis stood. His smile was back. Even under the dim flicker of the recovering lights, she could see that damn smile.

"Get back here, Hollis!" Metcalf cried, taking aim.

"Another time, Susan." Hollis ran a smooth hand through his hair. He acted like nothing fazed him. It was another trait she'd come to hate about the man—right in line with pretty much everything else about him. "Let's do this again real soon."

The doors closed, his smile the last sight she saw. Metcalf opened fire. Two shots slammed into the elevator doors but failed to penetrate.

"Count on it," she grumbled.

Steps approached behind her. Metcalf slowly turned to face a pair of guards. They leveled their weapons on her.

"We don't think so."

CHAPTER THIRTY-FOUR

The sound of fighting and gunfire trailed the elevator car as it headed for the roof. Four men surrounded Hollis, their hands at their holsters. They were paid to be prepared, even against the unexpected.

Tonight certainly fell in that category. It was meant to be a quiet party, an introduction to new potential partners in the Trust's work. Handshakes and false promises were the high points of the night, or would have been if Susan hadn't arrived.

Hollis couldn't stop grinning, bemused by the turn of events. Her entrance proved the theory that the DSA was still active. The rumors had started soon after the incident at the Cove, but the Nixon Jessup debacle cemented the DSA's revival. Metcalf's faked demise was a surprise, but a welcome one. It always paid to know your enemy, and Hollis knew Susan very well.

The elevator opened to the roof. Hollis stepped out of the car, and the wind threatened to bowl him over. The helicopter idling on the pad drowned out all other noises. His pilot waited, and he could make out a shadow in the rear.

Hollis turned to his guards. He yelled into their ears, "See to it our guests are all right."

Nods answered the request, but he wasn't finished.

"Oh, and find Mr. Duloc," Hollis continued. "I would like a word with him about what happened tonight."

"Yes, sir," they answered in unison.

Hollis stepped out on the roof to clear the way for them. All four settled in the elevator, their stances more relaxed yet still primed for action. Hollis didn't pay them to hold too many conversations, and if anyone had the privilege of having one with the guards, they would find out why.

Duloc had been played for a fool. The cause, of course, was that the man was, in fact, not playing at all. He was an idiot — an ambitious one, to be sure — but an idiot all the same. He believed his wealth made up for any intellectual inadequacies. But a checkbook was all he had provided since his recruitment to the Trust.

Punishment was in order for allowing Metcalf into the hotel, let alone for her infiltration of their secret lab in the subbasement. It was a setback, and there had been too many of them of late. The DSA continued to be quite the thorn in his side.

Hollis refused to let it weigh him down. The night air revitalized him, and he made his way to the copter with a confident stride. He opened the door and climbed inside. The moment the door shut behind him, the propeller noise diminished.

The pilot passed over a headset. Hollis placed the speaker over his ear, the microphone in front of his lips.

"Where to, sir?"

"The airport," Hollis replied. "I've had my fill of the city."

The pilot offered a silent nod, then set to work. Hollis could hear him communicating with Traffic Control. It was followed quickly with a word to his private jet to prepare for their arrival. Nothing was left to chance. There would be no more mistakes tonight.

The shadow waited to make her presence felt. She never needed to play coy with Hollis. Whenever he was with her, she took over the room.

"I hope you have good news," Hollis said.

The woman remained in the darkness of the helicopter cabin. Her lips spread, and the whites of her teeth shone through the shadows. "Of course." She held out a photo, her skin pale as it slipped from the darkness. "We traced a call to his wife."

"Where?"

"Missouri," she said. "A team is already in play."

"Good," Hollis said. He settled deeper into his seat.

The shadow leaned forward. "You look happy for a man no longer hidden from his enemies."

Hollis turned back to the hotel and his spoiled evening. "Susan was always going to find out." His involvement with the Trust had given him access to dozens of high-security organizations. It had granted him intel on the most classified of documents and situations. Still, his position at the head of the Trust remained a secret from everyone at the highest levels of power... until now. Hollis shook off the feeling of exposure, a disarming wave tossed to his companion. "Knowing my role means nothing. It offers her nothing going forward."

The shadow shook her head. "I'm not so sure. Metcalf is smarter than you give her credit for."

"Her duplicitous nature will be her undoing. It always has before." It had caused the schism between her and Sullivan. Her solo performance at the hotel had been nothing more than additional evidence in that regard. There was nothing to threaten the power held by the Trust—something he had built for the past two decades. Hollis, though, tired of the thoughts and desired a change in their conversation. "What about our other experiment?"

"Riley took the bait."

Satisfaction filled his face. "You knew he would," he said. "Good. When the time is right, we can use that against him and the rest of his merry band."

The shadow's gaze fell. She shifted in her seat, the confidence gone from her. In its place, a wayward stare reflected off the window.

Hollis' brow furrowed. "Does that trouble you, my dear?"

She hesitated but a moment. Slowly, a devilish grin filled her pursed lips. "Not at all."

Hollis nodded. He relaxed against the seat. "Good." He stared out the window. The night had not been a total loss. In fact, he felt it was the beginning of the end of his troubles with the Department of Special Assignments. "Very Good."

CHAPTER THIRTY-FIVE

"You're on the wrong side of this one, boys," Metcalf said. Lights flickered back to life in the penthouse. The two gunmen continued to keep her in their sights at all times. Metcalf slowly lowered her own weapon to the ground, then kicked it away.

"The winning side?" one of the men chuckled. His neck was as thick as a tree trunk, and his muscles bulged through his suit jacket. "Yeah, we're all right with that."

"If it means finally burying your ass, we'll take it," the second said. She recognized his nasal voice immediately as a CIA liaison she'd pissed off years earlier. Of course, there were many like him over the years and the name disappeared from memory, but the irritating sound of his voice carried through to the present.

Fingers poised on their respective triggers, Metcalf waited for the end to arrive. She regretted not bringing Kanigher, not even telling him what she had planned. That was always her way, the secrets and the lies — all for the greater good.

The elevator chimed. Not the one behind her, but the bank to the right of her position. The doors were slow to open. The arrival of the car, though, was enough to draw the attention of the two "gunsels" long enough for Metcalf to dive out of the line of fire.

She grabbed her weapon in mid-roll, then jumped to her feet to face the men. They shifted, sudden and exact terror in their eyes. It was the last mistake they made.

With their attention on Metcalf and their renewed standoff, they forgot about the elevator. From inside the car, black soles clattered along the tile floor, and a man in black stepped forward. Two shots resounded from the pistol in his hand, and the twin Trust agents fell to the ground. Their weapons spun free from their hands and scattered in different directions away from them.

Metcalf didn't bother to check on the pair. From the blank stares in their eyes, she knew they were dead the second the shots made their impact. There was no mercy for them. She certainly offered no forgiveness, considering what they had planned for her.

Instead, her eyes locked on the man standing just outside the elevator. He wore a black trench coat and a fedora. The moment his opaque glasses came into view, her mouth fell agape.

"You?"

"Hello, Susan," the Witness said. He tucked his gun away and raised his hands. "It's good to see you again."

"What the hell are you doing here?" she spat, weapon aimed for his chest.

"I had to come," he muttered. "They would have killed you."

"Like you care?" Dropping the gun to her side, she started for the elevator. She slammed her thumb against the call button repeatedly. She couldn't let Hollis get away, not when she was so close to the Trust's inner circle. "I don't have time for you."

"Make the time," the Witness replied. The controls dinged, and she moved for the open elevator. The Witness held out a hand to stop the doors from closing. "Wait, Susan."

"I can't."

"He's gone," the man said. "Hollis is gone."

Her eyes flared. "Hollis... You knew it was him."

"I did." Metcalf waited for more, her grip tight on her weapon. The Witness sighed. "Knowing about Hollis would have made no difference to what has happened to you or your DSA, Susan."

It was an excuse. The man always had them when it came to understanding his reasoning. None of them ever made it easier to swallow.

"What do you want?" she snapped at him. She hated him for what he'd done in Bellbrook, where seven thousand people lost their lives. Yet, he had saved Ben's life recently, causing her nothing but frustration at how to act. "You didn't come to save my life, or whatever other excuse you might come up with. So tell me, what do you want?"

"I'm not here for a fight, Susan." The Witness inched closer, his hands still in the air. "I came because something terrible has happened, and I... I need your help."

ABOUT THE AUTHOR

Lou Paduano is the author of the Greystone series of urban fantasy adventures, which follow Detective Greg Loren and Soriya Greystone as they hunt myths, monsters, and legends in the city of Portents.

He is also the author of the conspiracy thriller series, The DSA, a serialized tale about a clandestine government agency trying to discover the true power behind humanity's future.

Lou lives with his wife and three daughters in Grand Island, NY. You can learn more about his books, including upcoming releases and free content by visiting his website at loupaduano.com.

GREYSTONE-IN-TRAINING

AVAILABLE NOW

For years, Soriya trained to become the Greystone.
Follow the trials that made her the protector
Portents needed to fend off the darkest of threats.

BOOK ONE - HAMMER AND ANVIL
BOOK TWO - THE GIFTS OF KALI
BOOK THREE - THE FINAL GAUNTLET

THE DSA CONTINUES IN…

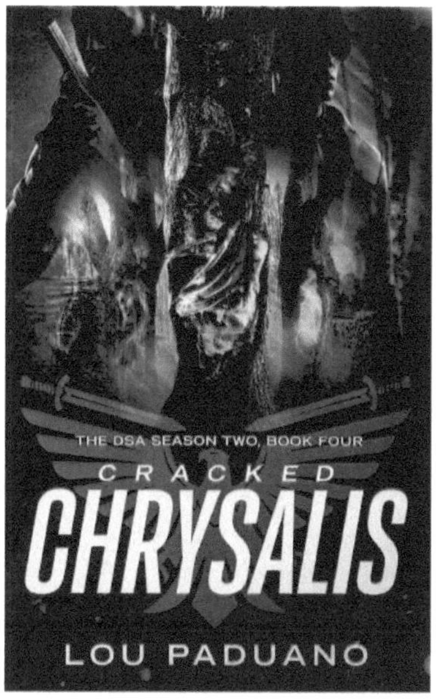

Ever since his deadly experiment on the unsuspecting innocents of Bellbrook, the Witness has plagued the DSA. He has cost them dearly with each interaction—including his role in the death of one of their own agents.

Now the Witness is asking for the DSA's help.

The next stage of his terrifying plan has been unleashed, only this time it is not by the Witness' hand or with his knowledge. Another dangerous foe from the DSA's past has subverted the products of his Bellbrook experiment and set them upon a deadly game. One that threatens a CDC facility and the viral contents locked within.

The DSA faces its most deadly challenge yet as the second season of the epic series marches on.